Mustang Mountain

Wild Horse

Sharon Siamon

Other Mustang Mountain titles:

Mustang Mountain

Wild Horse

Sharon Siamon

EGMONT

EGMONT

We bring stories to life

To Anne

Wild Horse first published by Whitecap Books 2003
This edition published 2009
by Egmont UK Limited
239 Kensington High Street
London W8 6SA

Text copyright © 2003 Sharon Siamon
Cover photography © Xiao Li / Shutterstock
© Alexia Khruscheva / Shutterstock
© PhotoSky 4t com
© Galyna Andrushko
© Plush Studios
© Mark Andersen
© Mike Norton
© Visions of America, LLC / Alamy
© Tom Fullum

The moral rights of the author and cover illustrator
have been asserted

ISBN 978 1 4052 4309 4

1 3 5 7 9 10 8 6 4 2

A CIP catalogue record for this title is available
from the British Library

Typeset by Avon DataSet Ltd, Bidford on Avon, Warwickshire

Printed and bound in Great Britain by the CPI Group

CONTENTS

Chapter 1

BATTLES

The sleek black sports car pulled up outside the Blue Barn Stables. The doors opened and four people got out – two of them very squished from riding in the back seat.

Alison Chant and her mother paid no attention to the sadly rumpled pair who wriggled out behind them. They were too busy fighting.

Both were tall and dark, both had straight

backs and straight noses. Both were furious. Alison wore riding clothes, slim boots, close-fitting pants, a trim riding jacket. An expensive black riding helmet swung from her hand. Her mother, Marion, was dressed in a neat, well-fitted black suit. They could almost have been sisters, except there was a sag to Alison's young shoulders that didn't match her mother's stiff posture.

'You didn't prepare for the district finals properly, and you know it!' Marion Chant's tone was frigid.

'Oh, well as far as you're concerned, nothing is good enough. It wouldn't matter if I was out here riding twenty-four hours a day, it still wouldn't be enough.'

Becky Sandersen, Alison's cousin, and their friend Meg O'Donnell, exchanged embarrassed glances. 'C'mon,' Becky whispered, 'let's just go in.'

They gave a backwards, sympathetic glance at

Alison, as they headed for the stable door at Blue Barns.

'Sometimes I feel almost sorry for Alison.' Becky shook her honey-blonde curls. 'My Aunt Marion can be harsh.'

Becky and Alison were first cousins, and both were fourteen, but it would be hard to imagine two girls more different. Becky had grown up on ranches in the Rocky Mountains. She was lean and strong from fresh air and living outdoors. Her hair was blonde, instead of dark and her brown eyes seemed flecked with sunlight.

'I wish my aunt would just let up on Alison about the dressage competitions,' Becky sighed, as she and Meg headed for the tack room. 'Aunt Marion takes everything so seriously. Since I got here, two months ago, I don't think I've ever really heard her laugh. She hardly even smiles, just walks around with that sarcastic smirk on her face.'

Meg nodded. 'She's totally different from your

mom.' Meg had come to love Becky's mom, Laurie Sandersen, when she and Alison visited Becky's home in the Alberta Rockies. 'You must miss her.'

Becky gave a quick glance at the tall girl with the wide blue eyes that missed nothing. How typical of Meg to realise how homesick she was feeling. In fact, life with her aunt and uncle here in this suburb of New York would be next to unbearable without Meg. 'I even miss Mustang Mountain Ranch,' she said with a shaky laugh. 'Who would have thought I'd ever say that?'

When her parents had moved to the isolated Rocky Mountain ranch, Becky had thought her life had ended. Being thirteen in a place with no friends, towns, not even roads or a school was like a sentence. Then Alison and Meg had arrived, suddenly and unexpectedly. Over the past two summers, the three had become so close that Becky had come back to school with them for the winter.

Last autumn it had seemed like a perfect solution, Becky thought with a sigh, but this year was different. It was going to be a long, cold winter living in Alison's big stone house by the Hudson River with Alison like a black cloud, fighting her parents every step of the way.

Becky took her bridle off its hook and started for the tack room door just in time to see Alison stomp into the barn, her face slammed shut like a book. 'I'm not riding at all today, then,' she shouted over her shoulder to her mother. 'If you don't like it, that's too bad.' She strode down the central hall of the barn to her horse Duchess's stall and disappeared inside.

Becky exchanged a worried glance with Meg. What would happen now? They could hear Alison's mother talking to the stable owner in a low voice. 'I don't know what I'm going to do with her, Virginia. Roger and I are thinking of selling Duchess.'

Now the look Becky and Meg shared was one

of horror. Sell Duchess! Alison might be spoiled
and difficult, she might rebel against her
mother's constant demands to win trophies, but
she loved her beautiful champion mare.

The stable owner's voice was equally low, but
calmer. 'She's a lovely horse.'

'Yes, and she deserves the kind of rider who
will put her best effort into winning, not
someone who can't be bothered half the time.'

'I'm sure Alison does her best,' they heard
Virginia murmur.

'That's just it.' Marion Chant's voice had an icy
edge. 'She absolutely does not do her best. The
horse is worth over fifty thousand dollars. It's not
a good investment if Alison is not going to take
competition seriously.'

'Development in dressage has its plateaus. Like
every other kind of learning,' they could hear
Virginia say.

'Of course, but this has nothing to do with a
learning plateau. Alison's attitude is the problem.

We see it at home, in a thousand ways. She's lazy, rude and inconsiderate. I don't know what we're going to do with her!' There was a pause. 'I haven't decided yet, but if you hear of anyone looking for a good dressage horse, I hope you'll let me know.'

The two voices moved out of earshot. Becky and Meg gaped at each other. 'She wouldn't really sell Duchess?' Meg's blue eyes were troubled.

'She might.' Becky made a face. 'She might just do it to punish Alison.'

Alone with her horse, Alison took a couple of deep breaths, not wanting to frighten Duchess with her anger and frustration. 'How are you, old girl?' she whispered, leaning her head against Duchess's warm horse-fragrant cheek.

Duchess blew softly through her great nostrils and tossed her head gently, as if to answer. She was a big horse, almost sixteen hands and strongly built, a Dutch warmblood. Alison knew she was lucky to have such a magnificent animal, but it wasn't Duchess's breeding and training she loved, it was the way Duchess nickered a 'hello' when she saw her, followed her in the paddock without being led, and seemed to know how she was feeling, like now.

'My mother thinks I don't try,' Alison whispered, brushing Duchess's forelock back and massaging the small white blaze on her forehead. But we know better, don't we, Dutch?' She remembered with a spurt of bitter anger, how it had been at that last dressage event. Duchess had not been feeling her best. As soon as Alison mounted her, she could feel that the mare was slightly 'off', not really sick, but just not able to focus. She knew, right then, they weren't going to win, so instead of pushing the big horse, she just lay back, gave her some slack and decided to enjoy the day.

They'd done a respectable job, and came fifth.

But of course, that wasn't good enough for her mother!

Alison reached in her kit bag for a soft brush and began to gently brush Duchess's glossy hide in circular strokes. It soothed the anger she felt remembering her mother's scorching words after the results were announced. It was no use telling her Duchess hadn't been feeling her best. 'You have to push her!' Marion Chant had raged in front of everybody. 'She's not a pet, she's a champion, and you have to make her be her best at all times, not just when she wants to win. Haven't I taught you anything?'

Yes, Alison thought bitterly, working her brush down Duchess's flank. You've taught me winning is the only thing that matters. Last summer, out at Mustang Mountain Ranch, she'd learned that other things were important – such as being kind to Duchess when she wasn't at the top of her form. That new Alison had struggled to stay alive for a few weeks after they got back. But she could feel herself sinking into her mother's world again, where status and being the best were the only things that mattered.

'Sometimes, I really hate her,' Alison whispered to Duchess, ducking under her neck to brush her other side. 'If only Dad would take my side.' But her father was worried about business these days, and he and her mother were constantly battling. He seemed to have no time to even listen to her problems.

'If you're not riding, we're going home,' she heard her mother's voice say. 'I'm not wasting time while you sulk!' She looked up to see her mother's angry face.

'What about Becky's lesson?' Alison threw up her chin and faced her mother.

'She'll have to miss it.'

'That's not fair . . .' Alison flared.

'Well, you should have thought of that! Is it fair that I interrupt my day to drive you all the way out here for nothing?' They glared at each other, neither giving in, then Alison turned away with a careless shrug.

'Goodbye, Dutch,' she murmured, kissing Duchess on the side of her head, and giving her face a last rub. 'See you Thursday.'

Meg watched the black Porsche turn down the stable drive towards the river and speed through the gate on to the main road. Meg could walk home from Blue Barns, but Alison and Becky lived on the other side of town, further along the Hudson River.

Meg turned back into the barn and walked down the row of stalls, stopping to rub the faces of the horses and working her way towards Duchess. The first time Meg had met Alison she was riding Duchess, right here at Blue Barns, and Meg had been awestruck at the picture of them. A perfect vision of a girl on a horse, like the kind of thing Meg had been reading about and dreaming about since she was a little kid.

She stopped at Duchess's stall and the big horse thrust her nose out in greeting. 'Here, girl, I can at least turn you out and muck out your stall.' She gave the aristocratic nose a pat. 'I'd exercise you, too, if I didn't think Alison's mom would have a fit!' Alison would have done that, if she'd stayed. One of the best things about Alison was the way she loved her horse. Meg could no more imagine her without Duchess than . . . than myself without Silver, she thought with a pang and a shake of her long brown ponytail.

Silver was gone. The gangly white colt she'd rescued in a snowstorm, the beautiful horse she'd loved and nursed back to health had gone – back to his home stable in Maryland. For over a year she had looked after him, loved him, helped his leg heal after an accident. It had been almost like having her own horse. Almost, but

Meg had known that she couldn't keep Silver, and she was glad he was ready to begin his training as a jumper.

She just hadn't counted on how much she'd miss him.

She clipped a lead rope to Duchess's halter, opened the stall and led the tall chestnut to the wide doors at the other end of the barn. Some day I will have my own horse, Meg thought. I'll get a job and save every cent and find the perfect horse.

The vision of a red mustang, galloping across a mountain meadow, leaped into her mind. On his back was Thomas, the boy who had captured this wild horse to be the foundation of his herd. Meg sighed. Thomas and his mustang stallion were far away in the Rockies. Someday, she might see them again. In the meantime, she could help out at Blue Barns and earn enough to help pay for her lessons, and spend her time with the school horses and the boarders, like Duchess.

'They couldn't sell you.' The sunlight gleamed on Duchess's smooth hide, as glossy and bright as a new chestnut. 'You belong here.'

go. I don't want to go. I'll tell her.'

Alison wheeled around and faced her. 'You wouldn't desert me on my birthday!'

'No, but maybe once you could have your own birthday party.'

'I CAN'T,' Alison shouted. 'Every year, I go, I eat, I get preached at by Grandmother Chant and she gives me a cheque for a present. There's no escape.'

She turned away and walked ahead of Meg and Becky, head held high.

'I'll bet it's a big cheque,' said Becky. She spread her arms wide and whirled around. 'Her grandmother Chant is rich. I wish you were coming to this birthday dinner, Meggie.' She stopped spinning and shoved a strand of golden blonde hair back from her forehead. 'Everything with Alison's family is so tense. You feel like you're always going to say or do the wrong thing.'

'So you have to keep quiet and stay still?'

asked Meg. Her face crinkled up into a grin. 'That must be hard for you!'

'It's torture. I almost miss doing chores at Mustang Mountain every day.' Becky grinned back. 'At least shovelling horse manure and raking sawdust keeps you busy.'

They caught up to Alison at the bus stop. She was wearing her remote, aloof, I couldn't care less look. Meg had seen it before, and she knew Alison did care, she was just too proud to let anyone see. 'Don't worry,' Meg told her. 'We'll think of a way to celebrate your birthday for real on Thursday, at Blue Barns. I have a present you're really going to like.'

Alison's face brightened for a minute, then shadowed again at the mention of the riding stable.

The phone rang after dinner, while Becky was doing her homework in the big room she slept in at Alison's. It was really Alison's sister's room, but she was away at school in France.

'It's for you,' Becky heard Marion Chant call from the stairs. She sounded annoyed at the interruption.

'Thank you,' Becky called back, racing to the bedside table to pick up the phone.

To her surprise, it was her mom. Aunt Marion could have said!

'It's so great to hear your voice.' Her mother sounded far away. The satellite phone at the ranch had a weird pause between speeches, and you had to wait before you answered.

Becky felt sudden tears prickling behind her eyes. She took a huge gulp of air. 'Hi, Mom.'

'How are you, darlin'?' Her mother's voice had a slight western drawl. A wave of homesickness threatened to knock Becky over. She wished her mom had not asked that question.

'I'm . . . great,' she answered.

There was a pause, then her mother's voice

spoke again.

'Becky, I called because I've signed up for a course at the Central Wyoming College in the last week of October, a special one-week seminar, and I see on the calendar that you have a study week that same week. I was wondering if you'd like to meet me in Wyoming. You could fly into Cheyenne.'

'Come out west, for a week?' Becky shouted into the phone.

'I know it sounds crazy, darlin', but I miss you a lot, and I will be a few hundred miles closer.'

Becky couldn't speak. The thought of spending a week with her mom was just too wonderful.

'It's a little more than two weeks from now. I need to know pretty soon if you want to come, because I have to make plane reservations early to get the discount. But think about it, and let me know by Thursday.'

'I don't have to think about it,' Becky gulped. 'I want to come. I'm coming.'

'I know you'll have to study for your exams that week, but Cousin Terri-Lyn's spread is a good place to work. That's where you'd be staying.'

'Don't worry,' said Becky. 'I'll study for my exams before I get there. School's not too hard this year.'

'That's great, Becky.' Her mother's voice was starting to crackle. 'The signal's breaking up. Hey! Wish Alison happy birthday for me, and tell her she's welcome to come, too. There's lots of room at Cousin Terri-Lyn's.'

'All right, I will.'

'Bye, darlin'. Your dad sends his love.'

'Bye, Mom,' Becky gulped again. The thought of her dad produced another homesick tidal wave. She was glad she didn't have to keep talking. She hung up the phone and threw herself down on the bed, her face buried in the pillow.

'Who was that?' Alison burst in. 'It sounded like you were yelling into the phone.'

Becky sat up, her cheeks red with emotion,

WATERFORD NO CITY LIBRARY

21

her eyes brimming with happiness. 'It was Mustang Mountain. You know that stupid satellite phone.' She realised everyone in the house must have heard. Conversations, even the most awful fights in the Chant household, were carried on in low voices and hushed tones.

'Aunt Laurie?' Alison plunked herself down on the bed. Her snooty look melted into a genuine smile. 'How is she?'

'She's going back to her college in Wyoming to take a course – and she wants me to come and meet her. It's study week.'

'Lucky you,' Alison said.

'You can come, if you like.' Becky had to force the words out. She needed a break from Alison and her family. 'Mom says there's lots of room at Terri-Lyn's. She's the old cousin Mom stayed with when she was going to college.'

'I know who she is.' Alison rolled her eyes. 'No thanks. I've heard about Cousin Terri-Lyn.'

Chapter 3

Birthday Presents

Alison's father, Roger, was out of town on business on Alison's birthday, so it was just Becky, Alison and her mother who went to dinner at his family home along the Hudson River.

Alison's Grandmother Chant lived alone in the big stone house with lawns that sloped down to the water. Becky had never been inside before and as she walked through the lofty hall her nose wrinkled at the smell. Too much old furniture, she thought, and a hundred years of dampness seeping up from the river. Nothing in the high country ranches she'd grown up on smelled like this!

Alison's grandmother was in her sixties. Alison said she'd had a bad facelift. Becky had never met anyone who'd had a facelift before, but looking at Grandmother Chant you looked away quickly. Her thin body was stooped, but her face looked like a much younger person stuck on top. It was strangely shiny.

'There you are my birthday girl,' she swooped at Alison. 'Fifteen, and more like a Chant every day. Come in.'

They all filed into the living room, where Alison's presents were stacked on a round table. The table also held an enormous vase of pink and yellow lilies that smelled even worse than the musty odour from the damp basement. Becky sank into a large maroon velvet chair,

as far from the flowers as she could get.
Grandmother Chant paid no attention to her, but
as they went to the long formal dining room, she
felt the old woman clutch her arm.

'How are you, Becky?' she asked in her
hoarse, throaty voice. 'You look, if you don't
mind me saying so, just like your father, that
cowboy who married Marion's sister. What's his
name? Ed? Ted?'

'My dad's name is Dan,' Becky said, feeling
her cheeks turning red. 'He's fine, thank you.'

'We haven't seen much of Marion's family.'
Grandmother Chant sniffed. 'Too bad, I
thought your mother Laurie was a pretty
little thing. You don't look anything like her,
do you?'

Becky could feel Alison's mother hurrying up
behind them. 'Laurie and Dan live so far away,'
she said in a clear, ringing voice. 'They are too
busy at their ranch to come east, you know
that, Mother Chant.'

'I don't see why they can't leave the ranch to the help long enough for a visit.'

Becky knew that Grandmother Chant thought her parents were rich landowners. Alison had told everyone at school that her parents owned Mustang Mountain Ranch. Alison's mother had told the same lie to her mother-in-law. The thought made Becky twist inwardly with anger. What was wrong with working for the government and being experts in equine management? Everything here depended on money, where you lived, what people thought of you, everything!

'Of course your mother and father came to Marion and my son Roger's wedding, but that was sixteen years ago.' Grandmother Chant was peering into her face. 'Who was that crazy woman that came with them – that cousin of yours, Marion?'

Becky could hear icicles in Alison's mother's voice. 'Her name is Terri-Lyn Arbus, Mother

Chant. I'm sure we don't want to hear that old story again.'

Grandmother Chant's bony face cracked into a smile. 'I just thought Becky might be interested. She's probably never met the wild cousin from Wyoming.'

Becky knew she should keep quiet, but it was too late. The words were already coming out of her mouth. 'Of course I know Cousin Terri-Lyn,' she said. 'My mother lived with her for two years when she went to college in Wyoming.'

'She did?' Old Mrs Chant's eyebrows shot up as if to emphasise her disapproval. 'She was a disgrace at the wedding. Loud, impolite and unbelievably dressed.' They were moving up the side of the large dining-room table. Alison was already standing at her place of honour.

'It's my birthday, in case everyone's forgotten,' she said. 'Can we just drop the subject of my parents' wedding and Cousin Terri-Lyn?'

'She actually wore her barn boots into this very

room,' Grandmother Chant sniffed. 'I couldn't get the stench out of this carpet for weeks!'

Stench! Becky bit her lip. She looked quickly at Alison and her Aunt Marion. Why didn't they say something? Both of them were riders. They knew. The smell of a good, honest horse barn could never be as bad as this stinky old house. And anyway, they probably weren't Cousin Terri-Lyn's barn boots. They were probably her best western boots, shined up for the occasion.

Mrs Chant was a horrible old snob, and they were all, including Alison, afraid of her. Becky thought she had never felt so lonely as she did at this moment, not even when she sat all alone in a mountain meadow, surrounded by waving grass and wildflowers. She stared down at her soup, tucked her hair behind her ears and tried to blink back her feelings.

*

'Well, that was my birthday party,' Alison sighed, flopping down on Becky's bed. 'Fun, wasn't it?' She had been watching Becky's normally rosy face grow paler as the evening went on. 'It's even more fun when my dad goes. He and Mom usually have one of their fights.'

'Why do you go?' Becky sat beside her. 'You could say no.'

Alison reached in her shirt pocket and brought out a neatly folded cheque. She handed it to Becky. 'I go for the gifts. For this.'

The colour flooded back into Becky's cheeks as she stared at the amount written on the cheque. 'Fifteen hundred dollars?'

'That's right. A hundred dollars for each year of my life. Until I'm twenty-one.' Alison ran her fingers through her short dark hair and made a face. 'It's sort of a bribe, to make sure I toe the line.' She bounced up off the bed and paced the bedroom floor, waving the cheque. 'But it's my money and I can spend it however I like. Nobody can make you invest your birthday present.'

'What are you going to do with it?' Becky asked.

'Haven't decided, yet.'

'I have a present for you, too,' said Becky, rummaging under the bed. 'It's not worth over a thousand dollars, but I hope you like it.'

Alison opened the parcel, carefully wrapped in blue tissue paper. It was a large western bandanna, bright red, patterned with black. Alison gave Becky a hug. 'This is perfect,' she laughed. She tied it around her neck and jumped up to look at herself in the mirror over the dresser. 'Red is definitely my colour.' She studied her image. 'What do you think? Should I wear it to my next dressage event?' She lowered her eyelids and tried a devilish grin. 'Just to please my mother?'

'Alison, I wish you wouldn't fight with your mom about riding.'

Alison spun around. Becky's face was serious. 'What's the matter?'

'Meg and I heard Aunt Marion talking to Virginia at Blue Barns on Saturday.' Becky paused. 'She was talking about selling Duchess.'

'Oh, that!' Alison laughed and turned back to the mirror. 'She always threatens to sell Duchess when she's mad at me. She's trying to bully me into becoming Junior State Champion.' Alison's eyes narrowed as she stared at her reflection. 'She'd never really sell Duchess. She knows what would happen if she did!'

Chapter 4

SNAP DECISION

Meg lived in an apartment over her mother's accounting business on the main street of their suburban town. She had a little brother, David, and a golden retriever, Sam. Her dad had died just after David was born, eight years ago. Meg's mother was a good business manager, so they lived very comfortably, but there wasn't a lot of money for extras. Meg would have liked to live in a house, but as her mother said, it didn't make sense when they already owned the building and it had a perfectly good apartment upstairs, a backyard for the dog and a big maple tree.

Meg was sitting under the tree on Thursday after school, polishing the name plate she had made in woodworking class for Duchess's stall. It was almost time to leave for Blue Barns and her riding lesson with Becky and Alison. I hope she likes this, Meg thought. It's hard to get something for the girl who has everything. She gave the shiny name plate one more flick of the polishing cloth and traced the chiselled letters. It was all right – Alison liked anything to do with Duchess.

Alison approached the stable doors with a scowl on her pale face. She was determined to ignore her mother. She and Duchess could win if people would leave them alone. Actually, she thought, her mom had been unusually quiet this week. Like now, for instance. She'd dropped her and Becky at Blue Barn Stables and driven off without a word.

'Let's hack the horses around the track,' she called to Becky over her shoulder. 'Just to warm them up.' She could feel her spirits rise as the familiar smell of horses and hay welcomed them inside the barn doors.

The long central hall was dim and quiet.

At the far end, Duchess's stall was empty. It had been mucked out, and swept bare. 'Where's Duchess?' Alison wheeled to face Becky.

Becky shook her head.

'I'll ask Virginia.' Alison ran back down the barn and burst through the office doors. 'Where's my horse?'

Virginia lifted her head from her paper work. 'Alison. Didn't your parents tell you?' Her face creased into a worried frown.

'Tell me what?'

'Well, I don't know if it's really my business . . .' Virginia began.

'Virginia!' Alison was very pale. 'Tell me. Where's Duchess? Is she sick? What's happened?'

'Duchess is fine.' Virginia fiddled with the papers on her desk. She looked up at Alison. 'She was bought by a man from Nova Scotia,' she said. 'Didn't they tell you?'

'They sold Duchess? My parents sold Duchess . . . and she's gone?' Alison's head was spinning. 'I don't believe this.'

'I'm so sorry,' Virginia said. 'They got a very good offer for her, and they must have made a snap decision to sell.' She looked down again. 'Or, maybe they thought it was easier if you didn't know. The people came for her yesterday. She's supposed to be going to a very nice stable near Halifax.'

The enormity of the words sunk in and Alison could feel her knees shaking. 'They sold her.

She's gone. I didn't say goodbye, or anything.'

She turned and blundered into Becky. 'Let's get out of here.'

They collapsed on the green hill that sloped up from the barn doors. Becky's face was flushed with anger, Alison's as white as tissue paper. 'Did you know?' Her eyes flashed at Becky.

'No! Like I told you, I heard your mom and Virginia talking two weeks ago about selling Duchess. That's all.'

'Ever since we didn't win that last event they've been threatening.' Alison buried her face in her hands. 'They kept saying they were going to sell her to someone who deserved her.'

Becky kept quiet. She had heard the threats, the battles, and Alison pretending she didn't care, insisting that she wasn't going to be pushed. Still, it seemed unbelievable that Aunt Marion and Uncle Roger had actually sold Duchess.

Meg appeared on the far side of the track. She

waved and then ran towards them, a package in her hand. 'Alison,' she panted. 'Here's your birthday present at last. Hey! What's wrong?'

'My parents and that witch Virginia sold my horse!' Alison's voice was deadly quiet. 'They think they can get away with it – selling Duchess and not telling me.'

'That's awful,' Meg sank down beside them. 'How could they?'

'Easy!' Alison's dark eyes flashed again. 'I wasn't doing what they wanted, so they found a way to hurt me. The surprise was part of it – letting me come here today without telling me Duchess was . . . gone.' Her voice broke. 'They'll say it was because of the money, because Duchess was worth too much to waste on a worthless person like me, but it's not the money. Believe me, it's not the money. And it was no snap decision.'

'I'm sorry.' Meg reached for Alison's hand.

She jerked it away. 'No. They're the ones who

are going to be sorry. You wait and see, I'm going to make them both so sorry they'll wish they were dead!'

She got up and ran, heading for the woods at the edge of the Blue Barns paddocks.

Becky got up to run after her, but Meg reached out a hand.

'Better let her go.'

'Do you think so?' Becky's brown eyes were troubled. For all her teasing, she loved her cousin.

Meg nodded, looking after the slim, hard-running figure of her friend. 'It's a good sign she's mad and not just crying her eyes out. Poor Alison. Her parents are so weird. My mom and I fight, but she'd never do anything so sneaky.'

'Neither would mine. It's no picnic, living in that house.' Becky pulled up a stalk of grass and flung it away. 'I can't wait to get out of there for study week.' She looked down at the package in Meg's hand. 'Alison's present?'

Meg slowly unwrapped Duchess's shiny name plate. 'I can't give it to her now,' she said. 'It would just make her feel worse.'

Running through the woods on the wide trail where she'd ridden Duchess a thousand times, Alison willed herself to take deep breaths. Not cry. They couldn't make her cry. They were going to be so sorry . . . they'd have to buy Duchess back. She'd think of a way to make them.

Two hours later, she marched back to the barn where her mother was waiting with the car. Her expensive riding helmet and crop were gone, thrown into a steep ravine in the woods. Her dark eyebrows were drawn together in a fierce line. Without a word, she got into the car and sat staring straight ahead.

Alison's mother made a move to get into the car too, and then seemed to remember Becky.

She flung back her seat so Becky could get in and stood waiting, not looking at Becky or Meg.

'See you at school tomorrow,' Becky murmured to Meg, squirming into the tiny back seat.

Alison's mother got in, slammed the door and swung the car in a tight circle away from Blue Barns.

With a sigh, Meg turned back to the barn, where there were still chores to do, stalls to muck out, hay to be hauled. She would miss Duchess. That great, beautiful horse had been so much a part of Blue Barns, and no matter what her parents thought, she and Alison had been a good team.

On the grassy bank outside the barn was Alison's birthday present, still lying where she'd dropped it. Meg ran her fingers over the name Duchess and headed for the trash bucket outside the barn doors.

At the last second, she decided not to throw

away the present. 'I'm going to keep this,' she said out loud. 'It will help me remember Duchess. I wonder what she thought when they loaded her in the horse van and took her away, and Alison wasn't even here?'

Chapter 5

More
Decisions

'I won't need anything fancy in Wyoming.'
Becky was stuffing clothes into the corners of her
soft-sided duffel bag: comfortable old jeans,
warm socks, fleece pullovers and riding gloves.

'I wish I were going somewhere for study
week.' Alison stared at her image in the bedroom
mirror. She was satisfied to see the dark circles
under her eyes, the pasty whiteness of her

cheeks. It was two weeks since Duchess had been sold and she was getting a good unhealthy, caved-in look, without using make-up. Sooner or later, her mother was bound to notice.

'Why don't you come?' Becky rolled up her favourite wool sweater and stuffed it in with the rest. 'Meg is.'

'Really?' Alison turned from the mirror. 'Meg's going to Wyoming with you? When did she decide to do that?'

'When she heard that Cousin Terri had adopted wild horses and rides them on the open range,' Becky laughed. 'You know Meg and wild horses.'

'Somebody could have told me,' Alison muttered. She hadn't been paying much attention to Becky and Meg for the past two weeks, and now she felt left out. 'Where's she getting the money for the ticket?'

'Her mom gave her an early birthday, Christmas and graduation present.' Becky glanced up at her cousin. 'Air fare is pretty cheap this time of year, and it won't cost anything to stay at Cousin Terri-Lyn's.'

Alison shuddered. 'Money's not the problem. Cousin Terri's sounds like a nightmare.'

'Only if you listen to your mother and your grandmother.' Becky shrugged. 'I've been there, and her place is not that bad. It's just that she lives alone, doesn't care about housework and wouldn't have time if she did. She has seven horses and a job.' Shoving a last pair of thick socks in her duffel bag, Becky sat down with a satisfied sigh. 'That's it. I'm ready to blow this popsicle stand, as my dad says. Why don't you come, too?'

'I don't know.' Alison turned back to the mirror. The thought of getting away from this house was appealing, but she had spent her life hearing horror stories about her Cousin Terri-Lyn. Some of them must be true. 'Her shack sounds cold and uncomfortable. Where will you sleep?'

Becky threw back her head and laughed. 'It's not a shack, for Pete's sake. And it has a great loft, where we'll probably sleep on the floor, in sleeping bags. On second thought, it's probably not for you. Anyway, your mother wouldn't approve.'

'Who cares what my mother thinks . . .' In the mirror, Alison practised curling her lip scornfully. Then, suddenly, her eyebrows shot up, her dark eyes widened and she swung back to stare at Becky.

'That's it. My mother would hate it if I visited Cousin Terri-Lyn. She'd be so worried about what Grandmother Chant would think! The very idea of Cousin Terri gives her hives!' Hugging herself, Alison plopped on the bed. 'This is a completely brilliant idea. Wait till I tell her.'

'I don't know.' Becky was suddenly unsure. 'You'd go all that way to Wyoming just to spite your mother?'

'Of course.' Alison's face hardened. 'This is

all-out war. Anyway, I might not have to go. The mere threat might be enough.'

She reached for the phone and punched in a number. 'Grandmother Chant? I just thought you'd like to know how I'm spending your birthday present. I'm flying out to stay with Mom's cousin, Terri-Lyn Arbus, for study week.' She paused. 'Yes, that's right. The one with the smelly boots who came to the wedding. Isn't that nice?'

'What did she say?' Becky asked, as Alison hung up the phone a few minutes later.

'She had a fit, of course. Now watch the clock until my mother barges in here telling me I can't go.' Alison swung her legs up on the bed and sat cross-legged, facing the door. 'I'll bet it's less than fifteen minutes. That will give grandmother time to call my mother on her private line, and for mother to talk to father and get up the stairs. You'll see.'

Ten minutes and fifteen seconds later the door

swung open. Both Alison's parents were there. Her mother's face was as pale as her own, and her father looked stern.

'What is this crazy idea?' Alison's mother glared from Becky to Alison. 'What have you two cooked up?'

'Leave Becky out of it!' Alison flared. 'This was my idea. I'm going to Wyoming for study week.'

'No, you're not.'

'If you don't let me go, I'll refuse to eat, I won't study and I'll fail all my exams,' Alison's voice rose. 'I'll cause so much trouble at school that they'll throw me out.'

Alison's father moved forward, brushing his wife aside and coming into the room. 'You propose to spend your own money on this trip? And you'll be staying with your mother's cousin?'

'Y-yes,' Alison stammered. What was going on?

'Then I think it's a good idea to go,' Roger Chant said. 'It will give your mother and I time for a quick cruise to Bermuda. I believe it's actually ten days, with a weekend at either end.'

Alison twisted a corner of Becky's bedspread between her fingers.

'You think if you behave badly and give us enough trouble, we'll consider buying you another horse,' her father said. 'It doesn't work that way.'

'I don't want another horse,' Alison said. 'I want Duchess back.'

'That is utterly out of the question.' Her father shook his head. 'I thought it was a mistake to buy such an expensive animal in the first place, but your mother insisted. It turns out I made a tidy sum selling that horse. I have no intention of buying her back, even if I could.' He turned away. 'Marion, I think we should go and let Alison get packed. We'll make the travel arrangements for her, but she'll pay for it as agreed.'

Alison's mother stepped forward. 'You'll hate it at Cousin Terri-Lyn's.' She shrugged her elegantly slim shoulders. 'You'll see.'

Chapter 6

ROAD FROM CHEYENNE

It was already dark when their plane landed in Cheyenne, Wyoming, two days later. In the arrivals lounge, Meg and Alison hung back as Becky flung herself into her mother's arms.

Laurie Sandersen was small and trim, with fair short hair the same colour as Becky's but without the same shine and bounce. Her face was lined from many hours in the sun, but her smile was wide and warm as she welcomed them to Wyoming.

'Meg, it's good to see you, and Alison . . .' Laurie held out her arms. 'I was sorry to hear about your horse.' It was so typical of her Aunt Laurie to get straight to the point, thought Alison, no beating around the bush.

'Don't be sorry. I'm going to get her back.' Alison tried to sound more sure than she was feeling. As they had flown over the countryside that stretched between New York and the western plains, Alison had felt herself going further and further from Duchess. All at once it was real – she might never see her horse again. She realised that it was all about money. Her father had never wanted to buy Duchess in the first place. It was her mother's vision of Alison as a champion rider that had forced him into it. As soon as he saw a chance to get rid of such an expensive investment at a good price, he had taken it. And he did need the money – his business was in trouble and sixty thousand dollars was a lot.

'There will be other horses.' Laurie gripped Alison's hand.

'I don't want another horse.' Alison tossed her dark head. Her aunt's honest sympathy brought tears close to the surface. 'If I can't have Duchess, I'm never riding again.'

Becky and Meg exchanged glances. They were used to Alison's pronouncements. She'd been vowing that she'd never ride again for the past two weeks.

But Laurie Sandersen looked upset. 'You've come to the wrong place, then. I think there are more horses than people in Wyoming.'

The luggage had started to slide down the carousel. Becky and Meg collected their bulging duffel bags, while Alison waited for her stylish suitcase.

'Is it a long drive to Cousin Terri's?' Becky asked.

'A few hours.' Laurie put an arm around

Becky. 'Wow, it's good to see you.' She squeezed Becky hard. 'I think you've got taller in the past two months.'

'I'll soon be lookin' down at you,' Becky slipped back into her western drawl without even realising it. 'How's Dad?'

'The same as ever. He sends his love. And Jesse Martin says to say hello to all three of you girls.'

'Jesse!' Alison turned quickly from the carousel. Jesse, a cowboy at Mustang Mountain Ranch, was the best-looking cowboy she'd ever seen. He was six years older than she was, but that hadn't stopped her from falling hard. 'Is he still going out with Julie?'

'Well, it's really not my business to know the details of his personal life,' Laurie grinned. 'Or to share them with you if I did. But Jesse will sure be sorry to hear you're not ridin' any more. He thought you were a fine rider.'

'Oh.' Alison's eyebrows knit in a frown. Then she lifted her chin. 'Too bad. I'm not riding for

Jesse, or anybody.' She could imagine Jesse, sitting tall in the saddle, laughing at her talking like that. But he wouldn't laugh about losing Duchess. He would understand. Jesse and his black horse, Tailor, were partners.

'Here's your suitcase.' Meg interrupted her thoughts. She scooped up the heavy bag and staggered over to Alison. Somehow Alison was always looking the other way when there was something heavy to lift! 'You brought all this, for a week?'

'Ten days,' Alison said bitterly. She had a sudden flash of her parents enjoying themselves on their Bermuda cruise, while she was stuck out here in the middle of nowhere. Why did she have this feeling of being cleverly manipulated, as if her parents had won, and she had lost?

'That big suitcase is gonna look take up pretty much all the space in Terri-Lyn's loft,' Laurie said, as Alison clipped on its strap and wheeled it towards the airport doors. 'I don't know if Becky told you, but her little house doesn't have much extra room.'

They stepped out into the clear western air of the Cheyenne airport. They were on the high prairie with the Laramie mountains to the west.

Alison groaned to herself. What if Cousin Terri-Lyn's shack wasn't as bad as her mother said? What if it was worse?

Alison fell asleep in the crew cab on the long drive to Cousin Terri's place. Her small spread was on the outskirts of a town called Antelope City, population 300. Through the night, on almost empty roads, Laurie Sandersen drove her pickup truck over the highest pass on the transcontinental I-90 highway, past the twinkling lights of Laramie, and the smaller lights of Rawlins. There they turned north over the Green Mountains, through Muddy Gap and west towards the Wind River Range.

'I wish we could see!' Meg was too excited to sleep. She tugged her ponytail tight and peered out the side window. Out there, she sensed huge spaces on either side of the highway.

Somewhere, in that big empty space, were herds of wild horses. If it were daylight, she might even see them.

Becky rode in the middle, beside her mother, feeling the comforting closeness of her. She was dying to talk about life in New York, about her Aunt Marion's and Uncle Roger's constant fights, about Grandmother Chant and her bad facelift, but it would have to wait. Alison might not be totally asleep. 'School's all right,' she answered her mom's question. 'Meg's in some of my classes, and we all have the same lunch.'

'But I bet Rockcrest is different than the schools back home.'

'I don't have a school back home!' Becky tried to keep the bitterness out of her voice, but it was there. At home, on the Mustang Mountain

Ranch, they were in a remote wilderness area. The nearest school was a two-hour horseback ride and then a long truck trip away. If she were living at home right now, she'd be studying by long distance. It was one of the reasons she'd hated moving to the ranch, at first. It was the reason she'd been so happy to go back east to live with Alison.

'I meant, the regular schools you went to, when you were younger,' her mom said quickly.

Becky tried to think back to the schools she'd attended before they moved to Mustang Mountain. 'The biggest difference about school in New York is that everyone's the same.'

'You mean the uniforms?' her mom asked. 'I couldn't believe you even had to have the school crest on your socks.'

'Not just that. All those girls talk the same, and think the same, and act the same.' Becky forgot that Alison might be listening. 'Their parents do the same kind of jobs, and they go to the same

ski resorts, and the same islands for vacations,'
she went on. 'Alison tried to help me fit in. She
told everybody you guys were rich ranch
owners.'

Her mother stiffened in the darkness. 'She did?
I'll bet that was my sister Marion's idea. I hope
you set them straight right away.'

'No,' Becky sighed, 'It's not that easy, Mom.'

Meg had been listening. 'It's hard to be
different at Rockcrest. I'm a scholarship student,
and everybody knows what that means.'

'That you're smart?' Laurie Sandersen asked.

'No, that my family's not rich,' Meg laughed.
'They always let a few of us poor unfortunates
in. It's a good school, and I'm glad I go there, but
I know what Becky means. Sometimes the air's a
bit stuffy.'

'Well, you'll be able to breathe out here!'
Laurie down-shifted the truck, going up a steep
hill. 'One thing Wyoming has, besides horses, is
lots of fresh air.'

Chapter 7

Cousin Terri's Spread

Alison climbed out of the crew cab, shivering in the high, thin October air of Wyoming. So this was it. A single light over the door, a bare bulb, didn't reveal much of Cousin Terri's house. She saw a battered screen and scratched paint where the dog must have jumped up to be let in. Everything else was pitch black.

There were a couple of tall cottonwoods near

the house, their dry leaves rustling in the night wind. A dog barked at the next farm, and there was the nervous blowing and stamping of horses somewhere nearby.

'Terri's truck's not here,' Laurie said into the silence. 'Come on, we can just go on in and wait for her.'

'Look at the stars!' Meg's voice was breathless. She was standing outside the circle of porch light, head thrown back, looking up. 'There are millions of them. It's like Mustang Mountain, only the sky is so much bigger!'

'That's a prairie sky,' Laurie said. 'The biggest sky you can get. No mountains or trees to get in the way. Wait till you see it in the daytime.'

'Are we going to stand out here all night and look at the stupid stars?' Alison hauled her suitcase out of the back of the pickup and bumped it over the rough ground towards the one porch step. 'I'm cold.'

The door was unlocked. Inside the temperature was exactly the same as outside, close to freezing. Becky's mother flicked a light switch near the door.

'Ugh!' Alison said. The little room they stepped into was barely big enough for the four of them and their luggage. It was hung with outdoor clothing on pegs, and piled with boots and firewood. Through a low arch, Alison could see the kitchen sink and counters, old wood cupboards, and a curling vinyl floor.

She could hear her mother's voice, 'you're going to hate Cousin Terri's', pinging in her ears. She couldn't believe anything could be as small and cramped and plain as this house. Through another doorway she could see a narrow bed, with a worn quilt, and a desk piled high with books and a beat-up old computer.

'The fire's out,' Laurie Sandersen said. She pointed to a small wood stove with a black chimney that snaked upwards at a crazy angle.

'Becky, look for matches in the kitchen. I don't see any here.'

Dragging her suitcase, Alison followed Becky into the kitchen. It was clean, but bare, with another stack of papers and books covering most of the table, a single kitchen chair and an old armchair piled with more books. The chair faced sliding glass doors that looked out into the darkness of the yard. The room was freezing.

'Where do you think the matches might be, Mom?'

'In the drawer by the sink.'

While Becky searched for the matches, Alison stood, glaring at her. 'Where's the light?' she hissed under her breath. 'Where's the heat? Where's the dishwasher? Where's the microwave? Where are my brains for letting you talk me into coming to this place?'

'I didn't talk you into it.' Becky found the matches and brushed past Alison's rigid figure. 'You wanted to come,' she muttered in a low voice. 'Quit rolling your eyes and looking down your nose at everything.'

At that moment they heard tyres, crunching on gravel. Headlights swung across the sliding glass door in the kitchen. A truck door slammed. A second later a dog scratched the side door open and a voice boomed out. 'It's OK, Ross, we've got visitors, but they're family.'

A black and white border collie whirled around the little room, sniffing everybody and barking like an electronic toy.

'Quit that yappin'.' Terri-Lyn followed him in and enveloped Laurie Sandersen in a bear hug. 'Hey there, little cousin. It's good to see you.' She turned to the others. 'Sorry I'm late – my truck broke down, had to put in a new fuel pump.'

Becky gazed at her distant relation. Terri-Lyn Arbus was tall and narrow and weather-beaten as a fence post that had stood out on the desert for fifty years. She seemed even taller in a black cowboy hat and high-heeled western boots.

Becky glanced at her boots, wondering if they were the same ones that had soiled Grandmother Chant's parlour carpet fifteen years ago, on her one visit to New York. They were a deep-reddish brown, with so many layers of polish that they glowed.

'Hey, Becky.' Cousin Terri's hair was long and streaked with silver, and she wore it straight, pushed back behind her ears. Her dark eyes gleamed in a tanned face with deep squint lines when she smiled. 'You sure have grown since the last time I saw you.'

She stretched out a welcoming hand and Becky saw that even though she wore turquoise earrings and a neat silver and turquoise necklace, she wore no rings and her fingers were as strong and callused as a ranch worker's.

'And this must be Marion's daughter.' Terri-Lyn swung around to greet Alison. 'Welcome to Wyoming,' she said. 'About time you made a visit to where your mother was born.'

Alison was speechless. Whatever she'd expected, this wasn't it. Cousin Terri-Lyn filled all the space in the small room and seemed to suck the oxygen out of the air. Alison felt her eyes widen, and her mouth fall open.

'Well, if you aren't the palest lookin' long drink of water,' Cousin Terri laughed a short rough laugh. 'You look like a white grub that just crawled out from under a rock. Never mind. We'll get some roses in those cheeks before you go home. You're shiverin'. Let's get that stove goin'.'

Alison was shivering with anger as much as cold. Her mother and grandmother had been right. Cousin Terri-Lyn was rude, loud and awful. She couldn't stay here. She wouldn't!

'This is our friend, Meg O'Donnell.' Becky shoved Meg forward. She caught the warning flash in Alison's eye and knew they were in for an explosion if she didn't do something fast. 'Meg loves horses, especially wild horses.'

'Well, she's welcome, too,' Cousin Terri-Lyn

laughed again. 'She can see my mustangs in the morning, ride one, if she wants to.'

The look of pure joy on Meg's face made Alison gulp down her anger. Anyway, she was too cold and tired to insist on going somewhere else tonight. 'I'd like to go to bed,' she said. 'Where do we sleep?'

She winced as Cousin Terri threw an arm around her shoulders. 'You poor little plucked chicken. I guess it is late for you, with the time change from back east.' She pointed to a narrow staircase against the far wall. 'Up there. You three are going to be mighty cosy up in that loft. I hope you all brought your sleepin' bags with you.'

'No,' Alison twisted out from under her sheltering arm. This was too much. 'We thought . . .' she started to say that they thought at least bedding would be provided in this dump.

'It's all right,' Laurie Sandersen put in quickly. 'I've got sleeping bags in the truck. The girls will be fine.' She, too, had seen the furious light in Alison's eye. That look reminded her a lot of her sister Marion, Alison's mother, when they were kids and Marion didn't get her way.

An hour later, Becky's mom had driven down the road to her room at the college. Meg, Alison and Becky were squished into the loft, in their sleeping bags.

'I'll be up before dawn, seein' to the horses,' Cousin Terri called up to them. 'You're welcome to give me a hand, if you like. We'll go ridin' right after breakfast.'

Not me, thought Alison. She rolled over with a grunt.

Riding a mustang! Meg squirmed happily in her sleeping bag.

It smells like home. Becky nestled deeper, loving the smell of a wood fire, the heat that surrounded her like a hug.

Chapter 8

MORNING

Meg woke up at six the next morning. It was
eight o'clock, according to her watch. Wriggling
out of her sleeping bag, careful not to wake
Becky and Alison, Meg tiptoed down the dark
stairs into the chill of the room below. The stove
was still warm, and she stood close to it while
she pulled on her clothes and boots and fastened
her long brown hair into a ponytail.

The sliding door in the kitchen was a large rectangle of grey light. The sun wouldn't be up for more than an hour, but the autumn dawn was coming. Letting herself out the side door, Meg walked around the little house to the front. It was shivery cold. The dome of sky was turning purple and in the dim light, she could see Terri-Lyn's tall figure forking hay into a feeding trough on the other side of a wire fence. Meg felt a thrill of excitement as the large shapes of horses appeared out of the shadows, walking slowly towards the trough. She counted seven.

Ross, the dog, bounded up, barking. Meg squatted down to ruffle his soft fur. The ground smelled spicy with the smell of sagebrush and dry cottonwood leaves. Meg sucked in deep breaths, happier than she could remember being for a long time.

'Is that you, Becky?' Terri-Lyn called.

'No, it's me, Meg.' Meg stood up and walked towards the fence.

'Good mornin',' Terri grinned. 'The gate's over there.'

Meg opened the homemade gate a crack, squeezed through and fastened it behind her. Terri-Lyn's feeding trough was the back end of a rusted pickup with flat tyres. 'All right, kids,' Terri told the horses. 'Breakfast time.'

Meg helped pull handfuls of hay from the round bale, and threw them into the trough as the horses crowded up to the box of the truck, and lowered their heads to eat. It was still too dark to see their colours clearly, but she could smell the good smell of horses and hay, hear their big teeth munching.

'So you're the girl that likes wild horses.' Terri-Lyn's voice was low and friendly. 'Did Becky tell you there's going to be a wild horse auction this week, at Sage Creek?'

'No!' Meg brushed back a strand of hair. This was wonderful news. Why hadn't Becky told her? 'Would we be able to go?' she asked.

'Sure, I'll be there, helping to register folks. I generally go to see what's on offer.' Terri-Lyn threw another big bunch of hay in the trough.

'Will you be buying a horse?' Meg asked.

'Nope,' came the short answer. 'Have to sit on my hands, though, so I don't bid. There's always some mighty nice horses.'

Meg had a thousand questions. She'd read about wild horse auctions, where the government sold wild horses that they'd gathered up from the open range. She wasn't sure how she felt about that, but she knew they had too many horses for the food supply and it was better than shooting them, the way they did in the old days.

Becky woke second. She rolled over and sat up, starving hungry.

Meg was gone, Alison still asleep and the little house empty and silent. Becky shoved her hair out of her eyes. Pulling on her underwear, jeans and sweatshirt, boots and jacket, she headed outside, grabbing a muffin on her way through the kitchen.

As she stepped outside, the mountains of the Wind River Range lit up with morning gold. Becky stopped to stare at the snow-capped peaks. She drew in a deep breath of the fresh clean air and it tingled all the way to her toes.

I'm home, Becky thought. It didn't matter what side of the border she was on, Alberta or Wyoming. It wasn't flat, and it wasn't grey and she could see the whole sky. I've been homesick for the prairie and the mountains, she thought with surprise, when all these years I couldn't wait to get away!

On the other side of the fence, she could see her tall cousin, Terri-Lyn, and Meg smoothing down the side of a brown and white paint, and she could tell, even from this distance, that Meg was peppering Terri with questions.

'Good mornin', slowpoke,' Cousin Terri grinned as she came through the gate. 'Meg and I got all the work done already.'

'I slept in,' Becky confessed. 'I came to see if I could get breakfast started.'

'Hungry, huh? It's this high mountain air. I was just thinkin' myself it was time for a big plate of scrambled eggs and bacon. How does that sound?'

'Perfect!' Becky smiled back. Bacon and eggs were never eaten in the Chant house back east. Too high in cholesterol. Nobody worried about cholesterol on a ranch. She was home, all right.

Alison kicked at the sleeping bag that was wound around her feet. Why were her covers so tight, and the bed so hard? Her whole right side ached, and what was that smell! For a minute Alison couldn't remember where she was and then she heard Cousin Terri's voice and it all came flooding horribly back.

The smell was horses, mixed with bacon and scrambled eggs. She was in Cousin Terri-Lyn's loft and she would be here for nine more days, unless she did something extreme. What rankled most was that her parents had known all along how much she'd hate this. She'd been tricked, and maybe Becky had even been in on it. It was supposed to make her forget Duchess, but she wouldn't. Not for one second. The whinny of a horse came from somewhere below. The walls of this shack were so thin it sounded like she was sleeping in a barn. No wonder it smelled like a barn.

Chapter 9

MUSTANGS

'Three of these horses were wild – that little paint and these two red roans.' Terri pushed the nose of a roan gelding off her shoulder. 'I got the roans when they were babies. See how they follow me around as if I was their ma?' She rubbed the forehead of the other roan, a soft rosy-grey horse, with speckles of darker grey over his flanks.

They were both shoving in, trying to get as close to Terri as they could.

'What are their names?' Meg reached up to stroke the first horse between the ears. It was hard to believe he had ever been wild.

'This here is Tyke,' Terri-Lyn straightened the roan's long silver-grey forelock. 'And the one that's trying to get in my pocket I call Pricey.' She chuckled. 'Because I paid too much for him at the auction. There was another guy bidding against me, and the price just kept goin' up. I knew I should've stopped, but I wanted him.'

'How much?' Becky couldn't resist asking.

'Five hundred dollars.' Cousin Terri gave Pricey a pat on the shoulder. 'And he's the best trail horse I've ever had.'

'Five hundred? Huh!' Alison snorted. 'My horse cost fifty thousand.'

Becky and Meg stared at her. Had she forgotten?

'Now that is what I call a pricey horse,' Terri

said gently. 'Course you can't always put a dollar value on an animal.'

Alison turned away with a HUMPH!, and marched back towards the house.

'I'm sorry about my cousin.' Becky could feel her face flush red with embarrassment. 'She can be so rude.'

'I heard about her mare.' Terri shook her head. 'I guess we got to cut her some slack. It's a terrible thing to lose your horse.'

'She says she won't go riding,' Meg said. 'Won't ever ride again.'

'Now that's a shame. I was hopin' to take you girls up out on the sagebrush this morning. It's my day off, and I thought we'd just go look at some of the country. Loosen you up after your trip, and the horses need some exercise.'

Meg could feel her excitement turn to dust. She looked up at the sagebrush bluffs, beckoning at the end of the fenced land. In all her life she had never wanted anything as much as she wanted to ride those horses into that wide open landscape.

'We can go without her!' Becky's face was still flushed. 'I'm sorry she lost Duchess, too, but she's acting like a spoiled brat, and I'm not going to let her ruin this holiday.'

Meg's heart sank even deeper. If there was one thing that would ruin this week for her, it was listening to Becky and Alison locked in one of their fights to the death. Becky had been quiet all term, taking a lot of abuse from Alison because she had to live in her house and go to her school. But now she was back on familiar ground, and she looked more like the Becky Meg knew from Mustang Mountain – strong, outspoken and stubborn as a mule. Her brown eyes were lit with fire and her cheeks were dangerously pink.

'Well . . .' The laugh lines around Cousin Terri's eyes deepened. 'So that's how it is.' She looked down at Becky from under the brim of her black hat. 'I tell you what. You girls work it out. If Alison is happy to hang around by herself, we'll go out for a short ride. I don't think she can get into much trouble around here.'

'I'll go talk to her,' Meg said quickly. She ran swiftly to catch up to Alison.

'We won't be long,' she explained. 'Terri said a short ride.'

'I don't care what you do.' Alison tossed her dark head. 'Ride up to Yellowstone National Park if you want. Fall in a stupid sulphur pit.'

'Are you sure you won't come?'

'How many times do I have to say it? I'M NOT RIDING!'

Meg gave her own ponytail a yank. Sometimes Alison could make you crazy. 'All right,' she muttered. 'We'll be back soon.' She ran back to the horses. 'She says it's all right,' she panted. 'We can go.'

'OK. The saddles and tack are in that little shed over there. You take Tyke, Meg, and Becky, you ride Shoshoni, the paint. Saddle up Pricey for me. I'll just go have a talk to Alison myself, before we go.'

They watched her take long-legged strides across the pasture, scrape open the fence and catch up to Alison, who had flopped on an old aluminium folding chair outside the sliding glass doors.

But Terri went right past her, into the kitchen, and reappeared a few seconds later with two mugs in her hand.

'Is that coffee?' said Meg. 'Alison never drinks coffee.'

'I wonder what Cousin Terri's gonna say to her,' Becky mused. 'Oh, well, let's get the horses saddled. I don't care what she says, as long as it gets us out of here.'

'I don't drink coffee,' Alison snarled.

'Suit yourself.' Terri perched on the step outside the house. 'But you're sittin' in my chair.'

'Oh,' said Alison, getting up awkwardly. 'Here.'

'Thank you.' Cousin Terri sat down, leaned back on the old vinyl strips and took a long suck on her coffee. 'I do like my chair. I like to sit here and watch the morning light come up on the mountains, after I'm finished feeding the horses, and then at the end of the day I sit and watch it go down over that high peak. Of course, it will be too cold to sit outside before long, but then I just move my chair inside and it works fine. I do love my mountains.'

What was all this about? Alison wondered. Who cared where she sat, and what she watched. What kind of game was this?

'Course you're welcome to sit here while we're gone, and I'd appreciate it if you could answer my phone, and keep an eye on the place.'

'O–kay,' Alison said cautiously.

Terri-Lyn gulped the rest of her coffee and stood up, hitching down her trouser legs. 'And if you go off the place, just keep an eye out for rattlesnakes,' she said over her shoulder as she walked away. 'They like to hide on the sunny sides of rocks.'

Alison stood watching her, her hands on her hips. Was that IT? Watch out for rattlesnakes and welcome to my chair? A stupid broken down old folding chair that looked like a relic from a garage sale? The way Terri talked about it, it could have been a solid teak heirloom. Her mother would have laughed! Alison wanted to cry. She watched Meg and Becky mount up and ride through the gate. Cousin Terri led Pricey through, closed the gate and swung a leg over Pricey's saddle.

She watched them ride down the dirt lane and turn off on to the open range. There were no gates here, and no fences. All three horses broke into a lope and went flying off across the sagebrush, long tails streaming out behind.

Alison sat down on the folding chair and watched them disappear over a low rise. It was going to be a long morning.

Chapter 10

ALISON'S WALK

After an hour Alison grew tired of sitting and poked around Cousin Terri-Lyn's spread for awhile. Besides the little house, there wasn't much to see. Two old cars that didn't run, besides the truck she used for feeding the horses. A fenced-in pasture, with no grass, just dusty grey dirt. The rest of the horses were at the other end of the pasture, clumped together near the fence.

No barn, just a small equipment shed and another shed for hay. Alison supposed Terri-Lyn's horses stayed outside all winter.

Ugh! she thought again. *Who could live here?*

Alison turned her back on the house and started down the lane. There were no other houses near enough to walk to, but she found herself walking anyway, with no particular goal in mind. She kicked a stone at the side of the road. *Rattlesnakes,* she thought. *Cousin Terri probably just said that to keep me from wandering off, and getting lost, the way my mother is always telling me to watch out for strangers.*

She turned and got a fix on the ranch house, then started off up the bluff. If she kept the house in view she wouldn't get lost. You could see so far in this country – it wasn't like heading into deep woods.

The bluff was longer and steeper than she thought. When she turned around at the top, the ranch house looked small and far away. In the other direction, the ground sloped even more steeply down to a little stream. It looked like a winding green line in a wilderness of brown and grey sage.

Alison found herself panting, and lightheaded. The water in the stream would feel cool. She would keep this big red rock in view and it would lead her back to this spot. She skittered down the gravelly slope, half running, and once again, when she reached the stream and looked back at the rock, it seemed small and far away. In fact, it looked like a lot of other rocks on top of the ridge.

The water in the stream didn't look good. It wasn't running fast enough to be clean. Probably just give me good old beaver fever, Alison thought. She'd had it at camp, three summers ago. In fact, she didn't feel so hot right now. Just the idea of beaver fever – throwing up and diarrhoea – made her stomach turn and her knees feel weak.

She shook it off and kept going, following a narrow path beside the stream. As long as I follow this track, she reasoned, I can't get lost. I'll just follow it back.

The stream and path led upward, into a narrow coulee. In places the trickle of water disappeared. Alison knew it had been a very dry summer and autumn, and the land was parched. 'I'm thirsty,' she said out loud, stopping to wipe her forehead, which was suddenly clammy with cold sweat. 'I wonder how far I've come?'

She turned and looked down the coulee, and nothing looked familiar. It was just an endless repetition of sagebrush and rocks, stretching out in all directions, and above that, a ring of low hills shutting out the horizon. She must have walked a long way.

'What is happening to me!' She was suddenly overcome with such a wave of sickness that she dropped to her knees. The sagebrush was rough and prickly and she had almost put her hand in the middle of a pile of horse manure. The sight made her gag and a feeling of weakness like she'd never had swept over her.

If she could just reach the water! She felt foolish and embarrassed, even though there was no one to see her – Alison Chant – crawling on her hands and knees like a baby. She scooped up some cool water in her hands and bathed her face. It did feel good. Now if she could just rest a bit, she could get on her feet and walk back down the stream . . . she curled herself into a ball of misery, her hand trailing in the water, and closed her eyes.

Rattlesnakes was her last thought before she blacked out.

She woke a few minutes later, and tried to get up. She must get back. She couldn't lie out here, alone. But she was shivering, chilled, and sitting up made her head swim. Just a few minutes more of lying still – then she'd go back to Cousin Terri's.

A crunching, rattling sound woke her up. A shiver of fear shot through her and she opened her eyes. It wasn't a rattlesnake, it was loose gravel scuttling down the dry clay bank of the stream. Something was moving at the top of the bank.

Alison blinked, trying to clear her vision, but the sick weakness inside made it hard to focus. Were those horses? Could it be Meg and Becky and Cousin Terri come to find her? A soft inquisitive nose was close to her left ear, and a hard hoof pawed at the gravel by her head. Alison made a move to sit up and felt the horse jerk away as if it had been burned with a hot iron.

She struggled to beat off the haze in her head. A sharp smell of horse, a flurry of heat and hooves surrounded her for a moment and then was gone. Alison looked up. Four horses were standing on the opposite stream bank, looking down at her. Two were white, one black and one a beautiful paint. They were facing her, staring, watchful, bodies tensed for action.

Alison sat up slowly, her heart pounding. These horses had long manes that hung in their eyes, long tails that almost reached the ground. No halters. They were wild, or semi-wild, and sending her a clear message. They were more afraid of her than she was of them.

A distant bark made them all wheel around, as if on a signal. The bark came again and the four horses exploded into action, disappearing in an instant, with the paint in the lead.

'Ross!' Alison tried to call. 'Come here, boy. I'm here.' Her voice was too weak to carry out of the coulee, and another spasm of nausea engulfed her. She sank back into her curled-up position, too miserable to care.

A few minutes later a sharp nose thrust into her face, and Ross was whining, urging, licking her. He sniffed at the place where she'd been sick. Then he was gone. 'Oh, Ross,' Alison groaned, 'you don't even want to help me. I'm too disgusting even for a dog.' Somehow, being abandoned by Ross was the last straw. 'I'm going to die out here on this desert, and nobody will care.' The barking had started again. Why wouldn't that dog shut up?

There were voices, too. 'Ross, come here! You know better than to go chasing off like that! One of these days you'll corner a band of wild horses and that will be the end of you!'

'Would horses really attack a dog?'

'Wild horses would, if they thought he was a coyote. They hate coyotes.'

'Look! There's something on the ground, over by Ross.'

'It's Alison!'

Now there was the sound of horses all around, Ross yapping in her ear, and Cousin Terri's brown face thrust close to hers.

'What's wrong? What are you doing out here?'

'I'm sick,' Alison mumbled. 'I was trying to get back.'

She felt a water bottle thrust to her lips, a hat jammed on her head, and strong arms hoisting her up. 'I know you feel like a dog's breakfast, but you have to get on this horse, young lady.'

Cousin Terri was mad at her! Was that fair? Alison felt her legs buckle, but Terri wasn't having any of it.

'Help me get her up on Pricey.' The strong arms were pulling her forward. 'I'll ride behind her.'

'What's wrong with Alison?' She heard a quaver in Meg's voice. Well, at least someone was sympathetic. She really did feel awful, and the idea of riding was impossible.

'Altitude sickness, most likely. She isn't used to hiking at 7,000 feet, and I'd be willing to bet she hasn't had breakfast.'

'She hasn't been eating for weeks.' Becky was holding her up on the other side, trying to walk her to the horse.

'And not drinking enough, either. We've got to get her out of the sun, and get liquid into her.'

Alison was tucked into Terri's bed. Becky and Meg were outside, sitting on the porch, facing the mountains.

Becky's shoulders drooped with disappointment. 'It's so typical of Alison,' she burst out. 'We were supposed to meet my mom for dinner at the college, and now we can't – why did Alison come out here if she was just going to act like a jerk? How could she wreck everything like this?'

'I'm sure she didn't mean to get sick.' Meg drew a figure of a horse in the dirt with a cottonwood stick.

'She never got altitude sickness at Mustang Mountain.' Becky shoved her fly-away hair behind her ears impatiently. 'I'll bet she's faking.'

The door behind them slid open. 'She's sick, all

right.' Cousin Terri's sharp glance made Becky squirm with shame.

'Matter of fact, if she can't keep any liquid down, we'll have to take her in to the clinic in town.' Terri shut the door behind her. 'Altitude sickness is no joke, as you'll find out if it ever hits you. Anybody who steps off a jet one day, and goes hikin' up a coulee the next could get it, especially if they're dehydrated.'

She collapsed on the lawn chair, thrust her long legs out in front of her and stared off into space. 'I think it's high time you two told me what's going on.'

'What do you mean?' Becky could feel herself blushing.

'Well, I'd say that my young cousin Alison isn't too thrilled with bein' here. Am I right?'

Becky nodded. 'I guess you're right.'

'Then why in thunder did she come?'

Becky took a deep breath, but Cousin Terri-Lyn went on.

'I was real happy, when I heard she wanted to visit out here, and I was surprised her ma was lettin' her come. Cousin Marion's been tryin' to live down her poor Wyoming relations since the day she married that uptight, poor-excuse-for-a-man, Roger Chant.'

Becky and Meg threw each other astonished glances.

'But right now I don't want to talk about Roger, or Alison's ma. It's that girl I want to know about.' Terri-Lyn was looking with narrowed eyes at Becky. 'I was hopin' there was some grit to her.'

'Oh, she's gritty, if you mean brave.' Becky couldn't help a laugh bubbling up, remembering the Alison who was never afraid of anything, who had fought off a grizzly bear, and survived a forest fire, and helped birth a foal out in the mountains on a dark night. She suddenly remembered how, before they'd gone back east, she and Alison and Meg had great adventures at

Mustang Mountain and felt like a team. It seemed so long ago.

'And she spent her own money to get here,' Meg added. 'Even if she just came to spite her mother.'

'That's mighty expensive spite!' Terri whistled. She got out of her chair and stood gazing down at Becky and Meg from under the brim of her black felt hat. 'The best way to treat altitude sickness is to go down to a lower level. Maybe we should just ship her back east to her grandmother.'

She grinned at the horrified look on Becky's face. 'I see you've met her Grandmother Chant. We wouldn't wish her on a one-legged weasel, would we?'

She slid the door open for them and said in a voice loud enough for Alison to hear, 'But from now on, we're not leavin' her on her own. We'll take her into town to see the doc now, while you visit with your ma, Becky. And if she doesn't have to stay in the clinic overnight, then she'll have to come to work with me tomorrow. I can't sit around here.'

There was a mischievous light dancing in her eyes that suddenly reminded Becky of Alison. 'Meg, why don't you help Alison get cleaned up and ready to go to town. Becky, come and help me feed the horses.'

Chapter 11

TRIP TO TOWN

'Meg, I can't get up, I'm dying.' Alison groaned and pulled the patchwork quilt up over her head. 'Can't the doctor make a house call?'

Meg pulled the cover back. Alison's face was as stubborn as a spoiled child's. 'Not likely. Not way out here.' She tugged on Alison's arm. 'Come on, Cousin Terri thinks you need emergency treatment.'

'She's not your cousin.'

'Sorry, I just don't know what else to call her. She doesn't seem like a "Ms Arbus".'

'It doesn't matter.' Alison tried to roll away from her. 'I'm not going anywhere. I feel awful.'

'You have to.' Meg tugged on her shoulder. 'You have to try. Your cousin Terri is talking about sending you back to your Grandmother Chant!'

As soon as she said it, she wished she hadn't. Alison's face turned green. 'No,' she gasped, with a hand over her mouth. 'I'm going to be sick again.'

'I don't think she will,' Meg hurried to reassure her. 'But, if you act like you're going to die, she'll believe you. When we were riding today, she didn't treat us like kids. She expected us to know what we were doing and she talks to us like adults.'

Alison sat up, threw back the quilt and swung her legs off the bed. She was still shivering. 'OK, let's go.'

'Do you want to change?' Meg supported Alison's arm as she staggered across the floor. 'Your clothes are kind of . . . dusty from lying on the ground.'

'Don't care,' Alison shook her head. 'Just want to get this over with. Can you imagine what Grandmother Chant would say if I got shipped back? I told you so! She'd carve it on my forehead.'

She stumbled over the loose flooring in the kitchen, but when Meg reached out to steady her, she shook off the help. 'I'm all right. I feel better when I stand up.'

Liar, Meg thought. But there was no doubt that her friend Alison had grit, or courage, or whatever you wanted to call it.

Alison lay on a stretcher in the emergency clinic, stripped of her clothes. She was wearing a thin blue sack of a gown, which didn't cover her or keep her warm, and they had taken away her socks and shoes. Where was that nurse? She needed a blanket!

The nurse had asked embarrassing questions about throwing up and going to the bathroom, that left Alison shivering with shame. Everyone in the whole clinic could hear! As if that wasn't bad enough, the doctor came and asked the exact same questions.

Alison's dark eyes took in the fluorescent lights, the harsh white walls, the sick yellow curtains around her stretcher and the small table with its Styrofoam cup full of lukewarm water and a bendy straw. There was absolutely nothing else in the room. Nothing to look at. Nothing to do.

She waited, listening to the sounds on the other side of the curtain. Low voices, moans, hurrying feet. The smell was strange and medicinal.

Every once in a while, the nurse stuck her head in the curtain and told her to drink. If she didn't drink, she'd have to have intravenous liquid through a needle in her arm and stay all night. When Cousin Terri-Lyn heard this news, she shook her head, and left. 'I hate hospitals,' she said. 'But you'll be all right here. Drink up, and I'll be back for you later.'

How much later? Alison wondered. What time was it? She would have got up and looked for a clock, but she was trapped without clothes or shoes. When was that doctor coming back? She'd show him she was fine – it was ridiculous to keep her here.

'Doesn't look like you've drunk much.' The nurse poked her head through the curtain. 'Are you nauseous?'

'No, I just don't like water in a foam cup. Have you got any ginger ale?'

'I have no orders to give you anything but water.' The nurse glanced at the chart in her hand. 'Guess it'll have to do.' She started to close the curtain.

'Wait,' Alison demanded. 'I need a blanket and I want to see the doctor.'

'Well, he's busy. We've got a broken leg, a kid with asthma and an old man having a heart attack.' The nurse's voice was flat, but you could have lit a match with the look in her eye. 'Drink your water. Small sips.'

Alison threw herself back on the stretcher and hit her head so hard on the metal bar at the top she almost cried out. This place was horrible. She had to get out!

She reached out a trembling hand for the cup and almost knocked it over. Holding it in one hand and her nose with the other, she sucked desperately on the straw. There! It was all gone.

Another wave of sickness made her curl up in agony. 'I drank it,' she moaned, hoping someone was near enough to hear. 'Bring me some more.'

*

Jake's Steak House was dark and rang with western music and loud conversation. Meg, Becky and her mother Laurie were just finishing enormous steaks when Cousin Terri-Lyn rolled in with the news that Alison had to stay in the clinic 'for observation'.

'Should we go stay with her?' Meg's blue eyes were full of sympathy. Poor Alison.

'Not much room in there for hangin' around.' Cousin Terri eased her long frame into the booth beside Meg. 'Anyway, there's plenty of people to look after her. She has to drink lots, the doc says, and take it easy tomorrow.'

'So, I guess we won't be able to go riding,' Meg gulped. She'd been looking forward to another ride over the sagebrush, maybe a chance to see wild horses running free.

At that moment a loud argument broke out at a long table behind them. A bald man wearing designer glasses was waving his arms at the waitress.

'Do you mean to tell me?' his voice rose higher. 'Do you mean to tell me there is nothing on this menu except meat? That you can't provide us with any vegetarian dishes?'

'Oh, he'd better not use the "V" word in here,' Cousin Terri-Lyn chuckled. 'This place is full of cattle ranchers. They don't take kindly to vegetarians.'

'That's the television crew that's filming wild horses, isn't it?' Laurie asked. 'I heard they were in town.'

'I guess they are,' Terri-Lyn sighed. 'We'll have them hanging out at the adoption centre all week, I expect. Say, are you gonna finish that steak?'

Meg shoved the huge plate towards her. 'It's the biggest steak I ever saw,' she grinned. 'Back east we don't eat this much meat in a week.'

'In a month at Alison's,' Becky muttered. 'Her parents are vegetarians.'

Terri laughed, her eyes crinkling up. She

sawed off a large chunk of steak. 'No meat, huh?
No wonder Alison's so spindly!'

'If you have to wait for Alison,' Laurie
Sandersen said, 'maybe we could go back to the
college. The rodeo students are having a practice
tonight. It might be fun to watch.'

'That would be great, Mom.' Becky's eyes lit
up. 'I'd like to see the college anyway.'

The field site for the college was a collection of
barns and corrals on the outskirts of town.
Pickups and horse trailers filled the parking lot.
Each student had to bring a horse with them as
part of the requirements. Besides the students'
horses, there were pens full of rough stock –
bucking horses, cattle, steers and calves for
roping events, and bulls for the bull riders. There
was a cement block building that housed the
office and student lounge, and a large indoor
ring for rodeo practice.

This is where Meg, Becky, Laurie and Cousin Terri-Lyn were headed.

'There's my young friend Wade.' Terri-Lyn introduced them to a slim young man in a pale blue shirt and wide leather chaps who was reading a list on the bulletin board. 'Hey, Wade, you ridin' the bulls tonight?'

'Yep.' Wade nodded. He looked nervously away from Meg and Becky. His eyes, Meg noticed, before his glance slid down to his boots, were a strange blue-grey, with a lighter colour in the centre. How could he be afraid of them if he wasn't scared to ride a bull?

'Good luck, we'll see you later.' Terri-Lyn patted his shoulder.

'You three go ahead. I'm going to call Alison's grandmother from the office phone,' Laurie Sandersen said. 'With Alison's parents in Bermuda, someone should know Alison's in the hospital, I suppose.'

'You're gonna call Grandmother Chant, that

old barracuda?' Terri-Lyn chuckled. 'Good luck, and don't say hello for me. Just tell her we'll take good care of Alison and we won't send her home unless the doc says we should.'

She led them out the office door into the large barn beyond, through the maze of metal bars and gates to a row of seats on one side of a rodeo practice ring.

At the other end of the ring were the squeeze chutes and behind them small pens where the rough stock waited for their events. An open door behind led to the barns.

The air was thick with dust from the ring, churned up by horses and cattle. It was cold in the big barn and the animal smell was sharp and acrid.

Meg noticed that the seats were covered with dust and grime. She brushed off a space to sit down.

Terri-Lyn chuckled at her. 'The dirt flies high when the action gets goin' in here,' she said.

'Good thing Alison didn't come,' Becky whispered. 'She'd never sit on these benches.'

The thought of Alison in the clinic gave Meg a brief pang, but Becky was right. She'd make a fuss about everything in this practice barn – the smell, the cold, the dusty air. 'She'd like the guys, though,' Meg whispered back.

The young bull riders were all male. They were gathered at the far end by the chutes, perched on the rails, lounging against the pens, waiting for the first bull in the chute. They all wore cowboy hats, and chaps slung low on their hips.

A young rider came up on a good-looking quarter horse. He raised his hat to Terri.

She nodded in return. 'Hey, Josh. You working on the horses for the auction this week?'

'Yup. How about you?'

'Yeah, I'll be helpin' to register people. Josh, this here's my young cousin Becky, from Alberta, and her friend Meg. Girls, this is Josh Mason, and his fine horse T-Rex.'

'Pleased to meet you.' Josh set his hat back firmly on his red-gold hair and nodded to the girls. 'Well, I guess they're getting started. I'll catch you later.'

'You know everybody,' Becky said, watching Josh ride T-Rex around the ring.

'It's a small town.' Terri-Lyn leaned forward, her elbows on her knees. 'Josh's a real nice kid. He's been volunteering at the horse auctions for a couple of years – wants to work for the wild horse adoption programme some day.'

'What's he doing here?' Becky had been struck by Josh's quiet good looks and shy manners. He didn't seem like some of the loud, teasing cowboys she'd grown up with.

'He's ridin' pick up. It'll be his job to steer the bull away from the cowboy and back into the pen. Got to have a good horse and be a good rider to do that job.'

'And be a little bit crazy,' Meg hugged herself. 'I don't know if I'm going to like this.'

Wade looked so small at the end of the ring. He'd put on a padded black vest as some protection against the bull's horns, but still! The bull that was coming into the chute looked enormous.

Chapter 12

IN THE CHUTE

The bull plunged and snorted in the narrow squeeze chute. The girls watched Wade lower himself on to the bull's wide black back. They saw him twist the narrow rope around his hand and give the signal to open the chute.

The bull exploded out of the chute with all the force of his 1500 pounds. As he plunged and corkscrewed, Wade was a blur of flying arms and legs above his back, anchored by that one hand twisted in the rope.

He lasted four seconds and then went flying sideways into the air.

Meg thought her heart would stop as he landed on his back, sprang to his feet and faced a furious bull twisting to attack his rider.

The other rodeo students waved bandannas at the bull and shouted to distract him. He swung his head, not sure where to charge. At that moment, Josh and his horse rode between the bull and the boys, herding the furious animal towards the pens.

Wade banged the dust off his hat and limped towards the rails. They could see his grin from where they sat.

'He'll be feelin' that tomorrow,' Terri-Lyn smiled. 'Nice ride, but a bit short.'

'How long are they supposed to stay on?' Meg's blue eyes were wide.

'Eight seconds, but I've seen championship

rodeos where none of the bull riders last that long. I think Wade's gonna be good. He's only just seventeen.'

'If you ask me, it's Josh who's good.' Becky's brown eyes had been following Josh and T-Rex. 'He's the one who saves them from getting gored or trampled!'

Alison wanted to tear down the ugly yellow curtains that surrounded her at the clinic. She wanted to scream, 'Look at me, I'm here! Have you totally forgotten I exist!' Where were her Aunt Laurie and Cousin Terri? Why had they just left her here, alone? Never, in her life, had she been treated this way!

Shaking, she reached for her boots, under the stretcher, and yanked them on. Her clothes must be somewhere. She had to get out of here, she had to go to the bathroom! Holding her gown closed behind her she wiggled off the high stretcher and pulled back the curtain.

'Where are you going, young lady?' A nurse poked her head out of another curtained cubicle.

'To the bathroom.' Alison swallowed hard. Her stomach was still quaking and her head felt too light. 'I need my clothes.'

'Not until the doctor releases you.' The nurse was brisk, but definite. 'The bathroom's this way.'

Clutching her skimpy gown , Alison scuttled for the door, her face red with anger and shame.

'Where have you been!' Alison whispered savagely to Becky on the way to the truck in the clinic parking lot.

'We went for dinner and had the most enormous steaks,' Meg began. 'And we saw a TV crew that's here to film wild horses!'

'Then we went to rodeo practice at the college,' Becky went on. 'We met these guys, Josh and Wade . . .'

'Great!' Alison's voice rose. 'The two of you are having a good time while I'm trapped in that hell-hole!'

'I didn't say we had a good time.' Becky tried to keep the laughter out of her voice. Alison was so predictable.

'Josh will be at the wild horse auction,' Meg told her. 'You'll get to meet him.'

'I couldn't care less about the auction,' Alison snorted. For some reason, everything Meg and Becky said made her furious. 'I saw your precious wild horses of Wyoming today – they were right next to me at the stream – and they're no big deal.'

'You saw them!' Meg stopped and stared at her. She'd give her right arm to see wild horses running free, and Alison, who didn't care, went for a walk and they came right up to her. It wasn't fair!

Cousin Terri-Lyn was holding the truck door open. 'Where did you see these horses?'

Alison could hear the doubt in her voice. She climbed into the truck and slammed the door. When Terri got in the other side she said, 'A band of them came down to the stream and sniffed me out. Then Ross's barking scared them off. They're just horses. Why does everybody get so excited?'

Terri-Lyn's long fingers beat on the steering wheel. 'You were lucky you were lying on the ground and they didn't see you as a threat.'

'They didn't seem very dangerous.' Was this like the rattlesnakes? Was Terri-Lyn trying to scare her again?

'Just unpredictable.' Terri started the pickup. 'It's not usual to see wild ones this close to town. Their watering holes must be drying up.'

'I can't move.' Alison was sitting up in bed next morning, drinking sweet tea from an enamel mug. 'Why don't you just go and leave me alone.' She sighed and lay back on the pillow.

'Oh, no.' Becky yanked the quilt off the bed. 'Not after yesterday. We're going to the wild horse adoption centre at Sage Creek, and you're coming with us.'

Meg came in with a plate of toast. 'Cousin Terri says Josh is going to be there. He's helping to train the horses as a project for his equine management course.'

'So that's why you're all dressed up.' Alison looked Becky up and down. Her face was bright with happiness, her hair shining. 'Where did you get that belt?'

Becky was wearing a braided leather belt with a big silver buckle. 'Terri-Lyn lent it to me.' She fingered the shiny buckle. 'It's from New Mexico, isn't it beautiful?'

'If you like that sort of thing.' Alison made a face. 'What are you trying to look like – a rodeo queen?'

'That's enough sarcastic remarks out of you!' Becky dived on to the bed, grabbed Alison by the shoulders and shook her so the tea splashed out of her mug. 'You have to wreck everything.'

'And you're getting breakfast all over my bed.' Cousin Terri-Lyn came to see what all the yelling was about. She stood in the doorway, her hands on her hips, her eyes narrow. 'Look, you three, I didn't bargain for shoutin' and yellin' and toast crumbs in my sheets. You either straighten up and fly right, or you're all out of my house. Do you hear me?'

Alison shrugged out of Becky's grip. 'They're always ganging up on me.'

'You're lookin' fine this morning.' Terri-Lyn strode over and took the tea mug out of Alison's hand. 'Get dressed, and be in the truck in ten minutes.' She turned for the door. 'And bring lots of water. There's bottles in the fridge.'

The three of them stared after her. 'Alison, we're not ganging up on you,' Meg mumbled when she was out of earshot. 'Can't you at least try not to be so miserable?'

Alison glanced from one to the other, with satisfaction. She had managed to make them almost as unhappy as she was. Meg looked like she'd lost her last friend. Becky looked mad, sorry and frustrated all at once. 'I really hate it here,' Alison sighed, swinging her legs on to the floor.

Ten minutes later Alison joined them in the yard. Her short damp hair stuck up in spikes and her face was pale and defiant. 'I'm ready.' She patted a lumpy packsack. 'I brought six bottles of water. Will that be enough?'

Terri-Lyn nodded, ignoring the sarcasm in her voice. 'Ross, you stay here.' She hooked Ross's collar to a chain. 'Dogs and horses don't mix.'

They drove up a long bluff and turned on to the highway. Up here, the desert spread out in all directions. 'It's all open range,' Cousin Terri-Lyn motioned with her hand, 'as far as the eye can see. Antelope, cattle and wild horse country, from the Sweetwater to the Green River.'

Wyoming, Meg thought, looked like a soft blanket of sagebrush thrown over a dome of high country, criss-crossed and stitched by tracks stretching off in all directions.

'What are all those roads?' she asked.

'Oh, some are ranch roads, some go to mines or oil wells, some are real old wagon tracks. The Oregon and California trails crossed this territory one hundred and fifty years ago, give or take a little. You put a road across this country and it stays put.'

Meg strained her eyes, trying to see horses. She saw clumps of antelope, with their white tails and golden backs, small herds of cows, black or brown, but nowhere anything that looked like a horse, not even a speck in the distance.

She could feel her heart beat faster as they turned into the road leading to the wild horse adoption centre, a collection of white pens surrounding a low barn. The steel-pipe pens were all shapes and sizes, from small and round to large paddocks. And here Meg saw her wild horses, at last. In the distance they looked like any other horses, clustered together, heads down, grazing on heaps of fresh green hay.

Chapter 13

JOSH'S TOUR

'I have paperwork to do,' Cousin Terri told them as they came into the Sage Creek office. 'That TV crew wants some background on the horses.' She glanced around. 'Josh, have you got time to show these three youngsters around?'

'Pleasure.' Josh tipped his hat. Becky noticed that the part of his forehead usually covered by his hat was much paler than the rest of his ruddy face. He was shorter off his horse than she'd imagined, but he still had that shy smile that seemed to tug at something inside her. Imagine being attracted to a cowboy! Becky laughed at herself. She had been so anxious to go east and get away from cowboys – but there was that smile again.

'What would you like to see?'

'Everything . . .' Becky gestured around the complex of corrals and pens.

'The horses,' Meg said. The old longing was strong inside her. All of these horses were up for adoption, and she wanted a horse of her own so badly.

'Sure.' Josh grinned at them. 'Let's go see the older mares with their foals, first.'

After the mares, he showed them the yearlings. 'These young guys are the most friendly.' Josh put one boot on the bottom rail and leaned his elbows on the top. 'If I go in the pen and sit real still they all get curious and start movin' towards me. Then one of them will take fright, and they all go tearing off.'

Alison lagged behind. Becky was eating up every word Josh said, and Meg was lost in a world of her own, gazing through the steel rails at the yearlings as if she could never get enough of looking at wild horses. None of them would notice if she just evaporated in the dry air.

She turned her back on Josh's endless lecture about the yearlings and gazed around the maze of pens. One had a partial roof, as shelter, she supposed from the wind and sun. There was a horse in the deep shadow under the shelter.

The horse stood with its head down, facing away from the fence. She was a paint mare, splotched brown and white. Her hindquarters were filthy with caked mud and manure. As Alison strolled towards the pen, the mare turned her head and looked at her with a wild, watery eye. For a second, Alison thought the frightened horse might bolt and hurl herself against the bars of the pen, trying to get away.

Alison gasped, suddenly remembering last night in the clinic, when she had felt sick and trapped. 'I know what it's like to be shut up in a small space and have strangers peer at you,' she said in a low voice. 'It's awful, isn't it?'

She marched back to the yearling pen. 'Josh,' she interrupted him. 'Why is that mare in a pen all by herself?'

'The paint? Oh, she has some kind of upper respiratory thing goin' on. Runny nose and all. Might be serious – might not. We're waitin' to see if she gets better in time for the adoption.'

'But why is she all alone? Horses hate that.'

'She might have something contagious. We don't want the other horses to get sick.' Josh tipped his hat back and scratched his forehead. 'That little paint mare's a real wild one. Scared of everything. Went ballistic when we had her in the squeeze chute for vaccination and freeze-branding. We were scared she was gonna hurt herself, so we didn't even try to wash her down. Then she got sick, so we put her in the isolation pen.'

Alison shivered, imagining the little mare struggling wildly to escape. She knew how it felt to be trapped, with no way out. She glanced over her shoulder. The paint mare had her head down again. 'No wonder she's sick after all that. She doesn't even look like a wild horse!' Alison thought of the proud, alert animals she'd seen near the spring.

Josh nodded. 'She's most likely missing her buddy, too. When we gathered these horses at Flat Rock, she hung tight with another mare that looked just like her, maybe a year older.'

Alison squinted up at him. 'Where's the other horse? I suppose you sent her somewhere else?'

'Might have,' Josh scratched his head again. 'The only way to tell is by checkin' the records. Date, place they were gathered, colour, stuff like that. I do remember the mare had one blue eye the way paints have when the white patch runs down one side of their face.'

'If that blue-eyed paint is here, and we put her with her sick friend, the sick horse might get better.' Alison kept after Josh like a dog with a bone.

'I suppose.' He shook his head. 'But we can't do that.'

'Why are you pestering him?' Becky tugged at Alison's arm. 'They have the sick horse in isolation – that means she can't have another horse in with her.'

Alison twisted away. 'Where are those records?' she demanded, never taking her eyes off Josh's embarrassed face. She had to do something. It was as if she could feel the mare's misery from here.

'I don't really know.' Josh shook his head. 'But maybe your cousin could help.'

'So where is Terri-Lyn?' Alison was almost dancing with impatience. It took twice as long for Josh to say anything as a normal person.

'She'll be at the end of the hall up at the office.'

Alison took off, almost running, for the long low office building.

'Wow, that's the most excited I've seen Alison get in weeks, about anything.' Becky watched her weave her way through the maze of pens. 'She must be feeling better.'

'You two are really cousins? You'd never know it.' Josh put his hat back on and watched Alison march away.

'You're not the first person to notice that,' Becky laughed. 'I sometimes have a hard time believing we're related.'

Meg said nothing. Alison and Becky didn't look like cousins – one dark and the other fair. One smiling and relaxed, the other so tense. But underneath they both had the same determined streak. They both hated to give up on an idea, once it had taken hold of them. Becky clearly

had her mind fixed on Josh. And if Alison
decided that horse wasn't getting a fair deal,
she'd try to do something about it.

Chapter 14

WILD PAINTS

Alison quickly found out that the paint mare with the blue eye was still here at Sage Creek. She was about three years old, and would be auctioned off with the rest on Saturday, the day before they left to go home.

'Would they ever auction the two mares together?' Alison asked Terri-Lyn. 'I mean, if they were friends.'

'Not really,' Terri-Lyn told her. 'They might put them in the same lot, especially if they made a nice matched set. People tend to go for the paints. But if someone wanted to just buy one, they'd separate them.'

'But that's not fair!' Alison protested. 'It's bad enough being rounded up, and penned up, without losing your friend.'

'Hold on.' Terri-Lyn took the recording paper out of her hand. 'It says here this horse is sick. She might not even be ready for the auction. You're gettin' ahead of yourself, little cousin.'

'I think she's just pining for her friend.'

'You may be right. And sometimes they just pine for their freedom, too. Some horses, it seems, would rather die than live on the end of a rope.'

'I'm going to talk to Josh again.' Alison headed for the door.

'Don't get yourself in a lather.' Terri-Lyn shrugged her lean shoulders. 'Josh's only a student. He doesn't have much say around here.'

'Who does?'

'Well, that would be Cliff, the head wrangler. But you better not bother him right now. He's got that TV crew on his neck, and he don't like extra people around with new horses. Spooks them.' She strolled back to her desk and sat down with a sigh. 'I suppose you're gonna go bother him anyhow. You plan to make trouble every day you're here?'

Alison stared at Terri-Lyn. 'I'm not going to bother anyone. I'm just going to find the other paint mare.'

Terri-Lyn got up with a sigh and took a battered cowboy hat off a hook by the door. 'Then wear this.'

'It's . . .' Alison wrinkled her nose at the battered sweat-stained straw hat. 'It's too big for me.'

'Well, you wear it, unless you want to stay inside here with me. That sun's hot and strong. If it's big, all the better. You don't want a dose of sunstroke, after what you had yesterday.'

Alison jammed the hat on her short curls, and gulped down the angry words that rose in her throat.

'That's better. I tell you what. I'll see what I can do about puttin' these horses in the same lot – that is, if the sick one gets over her runny nose,' Terri promised. 'You never know, someone might take them both.' Terri-Lyn shook her head. That kid would bear watching.

Banging the office door behind her, Alison tried to pretend she wasn't wearing a dirty, beat-up hat. The other three were at a far pen, where Josh seemed to be demonstrating his training methods in front of the TV crew. Alison headed for the large corral at the edge of the complex, where the young mares without foals were kept.

She found the paint with the blue eye easily,

but she was one of the shyest horses, and stayed as far from Alison as she could, keeping the others between her and the threat of this strange creature on two legs.

Even so, Alison could see the mare was beautiful, with lovely large dark brown patches of colour on a clean, creamy white coat. When she tossed her head there was a dark curved patch covering her ears, most of her face and muzzle, with just an eye-patch of white.

Alison found herself wanting to open the gate on the far side of the corral and let all the young mares run free. All their instinct must be telling them to take off across the desert, away from these pens. She watched them wheel and turn as a group, only to find their way blocked in every direction. At last she realised she was upsetting them, just by standing and watching. They saw her as a predator.

Walking slowly back to the isolation pen, Alison thought of the last two months. It was as if she'd been running against walls – no matter what she'd done it hadn't helped. Her parents hated her, she knew that, and worse, they hated each other, and used her as a pawn to hurt each other. And Becky and Meg had somehow bonded and left her out of their twosome. Even Cousin Terri-Lyn saw her as nothing but trouble.

Alison sat on a bale of hay near the sick horse's pen and took out a water bottle. She looked out over the low desert hills surrounding the Sage Creek centre. Wild land. Open range. She drank the water and tried to fight off the black clouds of despair that threatened to choke her.

'Drink, don't think,' she told herself.

After a long time, she heard the soft blowing of a horse, just over her right shoulder.

She didn't dare turn her head, or make any sudden movement. The sick paint must have come up close to the fence to check her out.

It was amazing. She hadn't run. She stayed by the fence.

Alison kept perfectly still, but started to sing, just under her breath, at first. 'Oh, give me a home, where the buffalo roam, and the deer and the antelope play.' She couldn't stand that dopey old camp song but now it seemed the right thing to sing, as she thought of the band of wild horses that had come across her yesterday, so much at home on their range land. The paint mare must have been just like them, before she was captured.

After another chorus, she slowly swivelled her head around and saw the mare blink one brown eye at her. Poor thing, she was a horrible mess. Her eyes and nose oozed an unhealthy discharge, and her mane and forelock were as matted as her tail. Still, she stayed close, as if Alison was a friend. No one else had been able to get near her, everyone else had made her snort and shiver with fear. She likes me,

Alison thought. She's starting to trust me.

Slowly, she stood up. The little mare didn't bolt – just looked at her with the same steady gaze, as if pleading for someone to understand. Underneath all the dirt, and clumps of matted hair, Alison knew there was a young animal, eager to live, wanting her freedom.

But the next morning, the mare was worse, her head slumped, hollows under her eyes. Alison was shocked as she approached the isolation pen. The paint mare quivered with alarm, then seemed to recognise her and pressed close to the fence.

'Josh, what's happened to the paint?' Alison raced to the round pen where Josh was painting lot numbers on the top rail, in preparation for the auction. 'She looks awful.'

'She's not eating.' Josh gave her a quick nod and went back to painting numbers on the steel pipe. 'She's given up.'

'But she can't,' Alison cried. 'Isn't there some way you can put the other mare in the same pen? Having her friend would make her want to live.'

'I'd like to, but it would be risking the other horse.' Josh shook his head. 'What she needs is to be adopted to a good home, where somebody takes the time and care to bring her out of it.'

'But that will be too late!' Alison stamped her foot in the dust. 'Isn't there somebody we can talk to?'

'Just Cliff.' Josh rubbed his chin. 'He's off with that film crew right now, but we can go talk to him this afternoon. I got to tell you, though, I don't think it's going to do much good.'

Alison fretted through the morning, trying to help Becky and Meg get packages ready for the auction: registration forms, vaccination records, information booklets and videos. The whole time her thoughts were on the sick horse in the isolation pen. She felt like the mare was counting on her. There must be some way that she could help.

Chapter 15

CHANGE OF HEART

'This young lady was wonderin' if we could put that three-year-old paint mare in the isolation pen with her buddy.' Josh sounded embarrassed to ask, Alison thought. That wasn't going to do any good!

Cliff was a short, barrel-chested man. He puffed out a big breath. 'You know we can't do that.' He stroked his long heavy mustache and glanced at Alison from under his hat brim. 'I'm sure you explained why to . . .'

'Alison.' She tipped up her chin. 'My name is Alison Chant.'

'Yes, well I'm sure Josh here explained that we have that sick paint in isolation, so she won't infect the other horses.'

'But she's going to die.' Alison held her ground.

Cliff looked startled. She could tell he wasn't used to having to explain himself to a skinny, pale-faced girl from the east who didn't know anything about wild horses. First the TV crew pestered him with all kinds of stupid questions, and now this! He puffed up like a bulldog ready to burst out barking.

'The vaccination we gave them three weeks ago should have kicked in,' Josh said quietly. 'The mare might be all right.'

'What would you know about it? College boy!' Cliff turned to bellow at Josh. 'We can't go bendin' the rules, just because some kid who doesn't know her britches from ditch water feels sorry for a sick horse.'

Alison could see Cliff was a man who had made up his mind and stopped listening. 'I thought you wanted to get people to adopt these horses.' She stuck her chin in his face.

Cliff turned from scolding Josh.

'I was planning to adopt both the paints, as a pair.' Alison glared at him, hands on hips. 'But of course I can't do that, if one of them is dead.'

She could see that had got Cliff's attention. His mouth fell open.

'You're going to say that kids can't adopt mustangs.' She stared him down. 'But I'm going to get my cousin Terri-Lyn to adopt them for me.' This was such an enormous lie that Alison nearly choked on it, but she was desperate. 'I'm betting that the mare won't get sick, and she'll help the sick horse get better.'

'You'd adopt them both?' Cliff looked at her as

if she were crazy, but he'd heard crazy things before from easterners. 'Why don't you just take the healthy mare? She's a nice horse.'

'Both of them, or nothing. We have a very well-equipped stable back in New York, where they'll have the best of care.'

'I heard about your stable, from Becky,' Josh put in helpfully. 'Sounds like a real nice spread.'

Alison crossed her fingers behind her back, the lies were getting so out-of-control. Blue Barns didn't belong to her, and it wasn't a spread, but an elite riding school. The thought of the two paint mustangs, scruffy and sick in that palace of purebreds, would make the owners faint.

But Josh's support seemed to impress Cliff.

'We sometimes adopt out animals "as is", no guarantees.' He stroked his handlebar mustache. 'All right.' He suddenly seemed to make up his mind. 'I hate to see a good horse pine away as much as the next man. We'll give it a try. Josh, can you catch that healthy mare?'

Josh was looking at Alison with wonder. 'Ah
. . . sure. I think so.'

'Well, do it then.' Cliff huffed and puffed away,
walking with the stiff, bow-legged stride of a
man who had spent his life riding.

The rest of the afternoon was a blur to Alison.
After Josh had managed to catch the mare and
put her with the other paint, she sat and
watched the two horses' joyful reunion on the
far side of the pen. They were a perfect matched
set, or would be, when the sick horse recovered
and got cleaned up.

Alison had no doubt she would recover. As
soon as the healthy mare whinnied, she lifted
her head and walked slowly out into the sun to
join her. The older mare groomed her friend
from mane to tail, combing her matted mane
and withers with her strong teeth. Then she
stood close, with her head near the sick paint's
flank and brushed the flies off her face with her
long white tail.

Alison and Josh watched the two of them walk to the trough to drink, and then to the pile of loose hay to graze. When the sick horse lowered her head to nibble at the hay, Alison wanted to cheer.

'See, I told you.'

'I'm glad you're gonna be able to take them both,' Josh said. 'The only thing I hate about this adoption business is when you know the people who take the horses aren't gonna be able to look after them right. They drive up in some beat-up old trailer, and you just know what kind of place they've got – busted down fences and mouldy hay.'

Alison said nothing. A trailer? Hay? Where was she going to get all that, let alone a stable? Even if Terri-Lyn somehow agreed to adopt the horses, how would she ever get them home? The pile of lies she'd told was getting as high as a heap of horse manure!

But I won't worry about that now, Alison told

herself. If the paint gets well, maybe someone else will want to adopt her. Maybe I won't have to.

'I got to go,' Josh apologised. 'Those TV folks want to watch me work with the horses.'

As the shadows grew longer and the sun sank towards the Wind River Mountains, Becky and Meg came looking for her.

'We thought you'd disappeared again,' Becky panted. 'Why didn't you come and watch the film crew? It's so interesting.'

'It's more interesting here. Look, now the sick mare's eating and drinking.'

'You've been watching them all afternoon?' Meg's blue eyes looked shocked in her sun-freckled face.

'Are you sure you're all right?' Becky peered at her. 'Have you been drinking enough water?'

'Quit nagging, I'm fine,' Alison sighed. She stood up and stretched, suddenly realising she

was stiff, hungry, and getting cold as the sun
went down.

'We're going back to Jake's Steak House for
dinner.' Becky danced beside her on the way
back to Cousin Terri's truck. 'And this time,
you'll be able to eat. Wait till you see the size of
those steaks!'

When Alison woke up next morning, the air
smelled sweet, her sleeping bag was warm, and
even the loft floor didn't feel as hard as before.
Last night Terri-Lyn had banished her back to the
loft with a laugh. 'I think you'll do fine, now.'
Her earrings swung as she'd tipped her head to
take a good look at Alison. 'I see a speck of color
in your cheeks.'

Alison lay there, watched the dust dance in the
sunbeams, listened to the sounds of Becky, Meg
and Terri-Lyn feeding the horses. She supposed
that she would have to tell Terri-Lyn about how

she had lied to save the sick mare's life. She was sure she could make Terri-Lyn understand. There was just no other way to save the wild horse's life.

Suddenly, she wanted to be sure the little paint was all right. She needed to see her. Dressing quickly, she hurried down the narrow loft stairs, through the sunny kitchen and out the sliding glass doors.

In the pasture, Terri-Lyn brushed down Pricey's flank with long, relaxed strokes.

'Hi.' Alison came over to pat Pricey's nose. 'You said this horse was wild, when you got him?'

'Pure wild mustang, five years ago.'

The paints might look this good, someday, Alison thought. She reached up under Pricey's mane to stroke the roan's neck. 'What time are we going over to Sage Creek?'

'Not today.' Terri-Lyn switched to the horse's other flank. 'I've finished all the paperwork for the auction. Don't have to go up there till Saturday morning at six.'

'Oh.' Alison felt a spurt of frustration. No matter what she wanted to do, some older, more powerful person always got in her way.

'Too bad you're not ridin' any more,' Terri-Lyn said. 'Today I was gonna take you girls up to Flat Rock to check out the spring. I'm worried that it's dryin' up.'

'Flat Rock?' Alison glanced up at her. That was where the two paints had been captured. 'Are there still wild horses up there?'

'Might be. They gathered up a small herd a few weeks back, but there's generally horses near water.' Terri-Lyn went on with her brushing.

'I . . . I might like to go.'

Terri-Lyn shook back her long hair. 'It's an awful long way to walk.'

'I meant, I might like to ride . . .' It took all her energy to force the words out. She'd made such a fuss about never riding again.

'On a horse?' Cousin Terri raised her dark eyebrows.

'No, on a camel. Of course on a horse!' Alison knew she was being teased and she hated being teased, and even more hated to take back her vow. She could feel Meg and Becky listening, behind her back.

She whirled and faced them. 'All right. I changed my mind. I want to go riding with you up to Flat Rock. Satisfied?'

'Delirious.' Becky grinned. 'Let's go.'

Meg's face glowed with joy. She grabbed Alison's cool hand in her own warm one. 'It's going to be fun,' she cried as they ran towards the shed where Terri-Lyn kept her saddles. 'We're going to see wild horses on the open range, at last.'

Chapter 16

UP CLOSE

Flat Rock was a steep-sided butte they could see far across the high golden desert.

'We keep riding, but Flat Rock doesn't get any closer.' Becky rode in front, on Pricey. She took a swig from her water bottle and leaned back to stuff it in her saddle bag.

In that off-balance moment, a fat sage grouse fluttered up from a clump of bunchgrass, right in

Pricey's face. He jarred to a stop and threw up his head. Becky clutched at the saddle horn. The grouse was the size of a turkey and the colour of sagebrush. A whole flock of them crouched low to the ground, almost invisible.

Cousin Terri sprinted forward on Rover, her bay horse. 'It's OK.' She gave Pricey an approving pat. 'Just a bird.'

She grinned at Becky. 'You're lucky. Another horse would have had you in the dirt, or taken off across the sagebrush if a bird flew in his face like that. But not a wild horse – they've got good eyes, and good ears and they're always on the alert. We just have to train them not to spook at stuff they don't recognise, like plastic bags, or rain gear that flaps around.'

'Is it hard?' Meg rode up on Tyke to ask. 'I mean to train a wild horse.'

'Not really, 'cause they're so smart.'

'Meg could do it.' Becky turned to smile at her friend. 'She has this amazing way of communicating with animals – like she gets right into their heads.'

Alison said nothing, but sat a little straighter in Shoshoni's saddle. Meg's not the only one who can communicate with horses, she was thinking. The paint mare trusts me – I could train her, if I had her.

She swept that thought aside and concentrated on riding Shoshoni across the wild, lonely landscape. Like the trail horses at Mustang Mountain, he made his own decisions about how to handle the rough terrain. It was so different to riding Duchess. Instead of focusing on the signals she was sending her horse with her posture, hands and legs, Alison could relax in the saddle and let Shoshoni do the thinking.

She felt a stab of guilt. How could she be so disloyal to Duchess? She had promised she'd never ride another horse, and here she was, enjoying this ride and wishing she had a wild horse of her own. Oh Dutch, she thought, I haven't forgotten you, I'll never forget you, but I know you'll never be my horse again. She suddenly realised that she'd never stopped to wonder, not once, how Duchess was doing in that far-off stable in Nova Scotia. Was she loved, was somebody looking after her? I've been selfish, Alison thought, with an irritable shrug. As soon as I get home I'm going to ask Virginia for the name of the stable, and call them and make sure she's all right.

Shoshoni felt the unhappy tension of his rider. His ears went back, and he tossed his head. Alison settled down and concentrated on the trail ahead. They rode on down a shallow draw, where the sagebrush grew higher and the pungent odour of sage filled the air. At the bottom of the draw was a spring.

It was called Settler's Spring after the wagon loads of settlers who had crossed this land on their way to the west. Water had meant the difference between life and death for those families, as it still did for the wildlife on the range. Now all that was left was a small mud puddle, surrounded by the deep tracks of wild horses, cattle and pronghorns.

A horrible smell filled the air as they rode towards the spring. The girls could see the half-eaten carcass of an animal sticking out of the mud.

Alison turned Shoshoni away, and put her gloved hand over her nose. Pew!

'This water's polluted.' Terri-Lyn got off her horse and walked around the trampled mud to the dead animal. 'A coyote or something killed a calf. Don't let the horses drink.'

She mounted Rover and they turned away from the sad scene. 'We should head back,' Terri-Lyn told them. 'I was counting on watering the horses here.'

Meg gulped down her disappointment. It seemed they were never going to see that herd of wild horses she'd dreamed about so many times.

But as they rode back up the draw, the sudden drone of an airplane split the desert silence.

They looked up to see a small plane flying low over Flat Rock.

'What's he doing?' Terri-Lyn squinted up at the plane. 'This is a Wilderness Study Area – planes aren't supposed to fly here!'

At that second another sound filled the air – the thunder of fast-running horses. They came galloping over the rise in a cloud of dust straight towards Terri-Lyn and the girls.

'Pull up your horses!' Terri-Lyn shouted. 'Stay where you are.'

Meg thought her heart would stop. The horses were headed straight for her, bunched around a snowy white mare with a long mane and a tail that streamed out behind her.

Becky pulled Pricey to a stop and closed her eyes. 'Steady, boy,' she cried, bending low over his neck.

Alison struggled to stay on Shoshoni's back.

He neighed with alarm, and pressed close to Pricey, trying to get out of the way of the thundering herd.

'Hold him,' Terri-Lyn shouted again.

Meg could see the lead mare's frightened eyes only a few feet away. Then the herd split and flowed around them, thundered past and kept on going. The plane roared overhead in pursuit.

'Get away!' Terri-Lyn shook her fist at the sky as if the plane could hear.

It was all over in a moment. The wild horse herd was lost in the dust from their flying hooves, the aircraft a silver blur against the blue sky.

'Well we got our wish at least.' Becky laughed shakily. 'We saw a herd of wild horses.'

'I wish they hadn't gone so fast.' Meg was still reeling from the sight and sound of the horses all around her.

'That plane started a stampede!' Terri-Lyn was red-faced with anger. 'If those idiots from the TV crew hired it, they're going to be mighty sorry they chased those horses. You kids could have been bucked off and trampled.' She rode ahead. 'Come on. I want to get back to Sage Creek and throw the book at them.'

Alison reached down and stroked Shoshoni's quivering neck. 'You were great,' she told him. 'You didn't spook, and you didn't stampede, you just stayed steady and kept us safe.'

'Wouldn't you love to adopt one of these horses?' Meg rode up beside Alison.

Alison glanced at Meg's glowing face. 'Meg, can you keep a secret?'

'Sure.' Meg rode closer so she could hear.

'I've done a really stupid thing.' Alison leaned towards her. 'I told Cliff, the head wrangler, that I was going to adopt those two paint mares – you know, my little sick one, and her friend.'

'But you're not old enough!'

'I know, that's just it. I said Terri-Lyn was going to adopt them for me. Bid for them at the auction. It was a dumb lie, but I couldn't think of anything else at the time.'

'Alison,' Meg gasped. 'What's Terri-Lyn going to say if she finds out?'

'I know,' Alison mourned. 'And it gets worse. I said we'd have them shipped back to Blue Barns.'

Meg stared at her. 'Two wild mares at Blue Barns? You are completely crazy.' She flipped her ponytail over her shoulder. 'But wouldn't it be fantastic if we could?'

'Sure. I'd have my mare, and you could have her blue-eyed friend. It's a beautiful dream, Meg, but it's not going to come true.' Alison slumped in the saddle. 'I'm going to get in trouble, like I always do. Even worse, I don't know what will happen to the horses. I wish that auction would never come.'

Chapter 17

TV Celebrity

While Terri-Lyn swept into the office to pounce
on the film crew, Alison raced to the isolation
pen to check on the mares.

The two paints were munching hay, swishing
their tails and looking content. They barely
looked up when Alison charged up to their fence.

The sick horse still had a bit of discharge from
her nose and eyes, but she looked happier, and

best of all, her friend showed no symptoms.
They might be all right, Alison thought, crossing
her fingers.

'Excuse me, are you Alison Chant?' a low,
silky voice sounded in her ear.

Alison whirled around to see the red-haired
TV host and her pudgy, middle-aged camera
person right behind her. Where had they come
from? And why weren't they up at the office,
getting chewed out by Cousin Terri-Lyn?

'How do you know my name?' Alison stared at
the host. The woman wore her fake TV smile, a
pair of stiff new blue jeans and a satin cowboy
shirt with fringe.

'Cliff, the head wrangler, told us all about you.
We understand that you, personally, saved that
gorgeous wild horse from dying of loneliness.'
The host sounded professionally heartbroken.
'We wondered if you'd like to tell us about it?'

'I guess . . .' Alison began.

'Fine. Hold it.' The host's voice changed from

sad to crisp in a breath. 'On me in five,' she told the cameraman. There was a pause as he got set, and then her voice went back to soft and low. 'We're broadcasting live from the wild horse centre at Sage Creek, Wyoming, here with the heart-warming story of a young girl wanting to save the life of a young wild horse . . .' She turned to Alison and flashed a big-screen smile. 'Alison Chant, the horses we see in this pen look so beautiful, but it wasn't always this way, was it?'

'No.' Out of the corner of her eye, Alison could see Cousin Terri-Lyn marching towards the pen, fire in her eye. These TV people were in trouble!

'You saw that the smaller of the two brown and white horses was sick, isn't that right?'

'Paints,' Alison corrected her. 'They're called paint horses.'

'Yes, fine. And somehow, you heard that this paint horse was separated from her friend, and the only way to reunite them was to adopt them both, is that correct?'

Terri-Lyn was two strides away. Alison gulped.
'Well, I . . .'

'But you're too young to legally adopt wild
horses, so you enlisted the help of your aunt . . .'

'I'm actually her great-cousin.' Terri-Lyn was
looking at Alison with a puzzled frown. 'What's
this all about?'

Before Alison could explain, the TV host
grabbed Terri-Lyn's arm and dragged her into
camera range. 'And here she is, the other hero
of this story. Terri-Lyn Arbus, who works part
time for the Sage Creek Wild Horse Adoption
programme, and has generously agreed to
formally adopt these two horses for her niece . . .
that is, cousin.'

The surprise in Cousin Terri-Lyn's dark eyes
turned to hot coals. She put an arm around
Alison's shoulder and grinned with gritted
teeth. 'We have a lot to talk about, Alison and
I.' She dug her strong fingers into Alison's
shoulder. 'We both love wild horses and fully

support the adoption programme, don't we?'

Alison nodded. She could feel the heat of Cousin Terri's anger through two layers of cloth.

'However, there are lots of details to work out. Technically, one person can't adopt any wild horse for another party.'

'Well, I'm sure you'll work it out. Has anyone ever told you that you look very much alike, you two? Just like the two paint mares that will soon be going to a wonderful new home, in New York State . . .' The cameraman swung his camera to focus on the paints in the pen, while the host babbled on about the horses.

Cousin Terri-Lyn looked down at Alison and waited until the camera switched off. 'We have a lot to talk about,' she repeated under her breath and then said to the host, 'I think there's a bunch of people lookin' for you up at the office. Something about photographin' wild horses from a plane?' Her voice was even, but Alison could hear the anger underneath, and Terri-Lyn

didn't let go of her until the TV crew had
hurried away.

'Now.' Her eyes drilled into Alison's. 'Suppose
you tell me what that was all about?'

'You realise there's no way I'm going to bid on
those paints at the auction?' Cousin Terri-Lyn
was pacing up and down her kitchen, her eyes
flashing fire. 'I don't care if everybody in the
whole country saw me on TV, I'm not bidding.'
She stopped and glared at Alison.

Alison didn't say anything. She looked down
at the checked tablecloth and the crumbs from
tonight's dinner of bread and stew. She wished
Meg and Becky hadn't left her and gone off with
Becky's mother.

'You can't just make up stories, and then
expect people will go along with them.'

'I know.' Alison looked up. 'I'm sorry I lied. I
was just trying to save the sick paint. I was

hoping if she made it to the auction, someone else would bid on her. That someone would take them both. Cliff said sometimes people take horses "as is".'

'Some people. Not me. I don't need any more horses. Anyway, it's time you learned a lesson. You can't have something just because you want it. How were you gonna pay for those horses? Or was I supposed to do that, too?'

'No.' Alison was stung. 'I've got money left from Grandmother Chant's cheque.'

'That's what I mean,' Terri-Lyn stormed. 'Your grandmother spoils you rotten.' She plunked down on a chair. 'That birthday cheque of yours is more money than I make in a month.'

Alison bit her lip. 'I'm sorry.' She looked around the small kitchen. It had looked so shabby when she came, and now seemed just simple and comfortable. Cousin Terri didn't own one single thing she didn't use every day, not one set of fine china, or a silver tea service or linen napkins. Nothing to show off, or impress people. Everything was real. Cousin Terri-Lyn was real. The worst part, she thought, is that she thinks I'm a spoiled, lying phony. If only I'd had a chance to explain first, before that TV person stuck a microphone in my face.

'The only silver lining,' Terri-Lyn muttered, as if she'd read Alison's thoughts, 'is that somebody might see that TV show and come to the auction, and bid on the paints. You never know.'

Alison nodded miserably. The auction was in two days. Then they would fly home and she'd probably never see the paint mares or Cousin Terri-Lyn again. It's just typical, Alison thought. Nothing in my life works out.

Chapter 18

THE AUCTION

At seven o'clock on Saturday morning, when the pickups and trailers started pulling into the Sage Creek parking lot, Terri-Lyn's truck had already been there for an hour.

Meg and Becky were excited and happy helping Terri-Lyn in the registration tent.

Alison watched people pour out of their vehicles to inspect the horses before the auction.

They picked up a list from the registration tent that gave the age of each horse and a brief description, and then headed for the pens.

The moms and dads discussed the horses' conformation and condition. The kids reached up to stroke noses, their young faces filled with awe. Young, whip-thin ranch hands prowled in pairs, looking for a special horse, their faces intent. Older people in warm baggy coats stood and chatted about the new crop of horses and all the others they'd known. Everybody, young or old, wore a big western hat. When the sun was fully up, it would be blazing.

Tiered seats were set up for the auction. In front of the benches was a small show ring where the horses would be paraded in lots, and behind that a raised stand for the auctioneer and officials.

The horses themselves were tied to the fence. In the early dawn light, their coats glowed – rich blacks, fiery sorrels, and all colours of brown and paint. The little weanling foals were grouped together, other horses were grouped by size or age.

Alison walked slowly to the pen where the two paint mares were tied to the fence. Lot 43 was the number painted on the white steel fence bar above their heads. They each wore a thin red cord around their necks to show they were mares, like a piece of cheap gift wrapping, Alison thought.

She parked herself in front of the paint mares. She would stay with them as long as she could, helping them face this new situation, all of these strangers poking and staring. Her heart felt heavy and sick. Part of her wished time would stop and another part that this would all be over.

After an hour she felt something nudge her back. It was Meg, holding a steaming mug of hot chocolate in each hand. 'I brought you one,' she said. 'I thought you might be getting cold, standing here.'

'No. I couldn't drink anything.' Alison waved the hot chocolate away.

'The auction's going to start. Becky and I will save you a seat.' Meg pointed to where the benches were filling up.

'Thanks.' Alison knew Meg was sorry for her, but pity made her feel worse.

She waited until the paint mares were led away, and then walked slowly to the benches. Becky and Meg were waving from a seat halfway up. Alison threaded her way through the excited crowd. She saw people pointing at her and whispering, 'That was the girl on TV!'

This was so humiliating. 'Where's Cousin Terri?' She squeezed in beside Becky.

'She said she's going to stay in the registration tent.' Becky threw Alison a sympathetic glance.

'She has to hand out tickets to people who want to bid.' Meg pointed to a man two seats away holding a square of brown cardboard with the number 21 written on it in large black marker. 'Maybe she'll come up later.'

'I doubt it,' Alison muttered. 'She's not going to bid.' Cousin Terri would hate people staring at her. I'd like to leave, too, Alison thought, but I have to stay and see what happens to the mares.

It was cold, sitting on the aluminium bench. Alison watched Cliff, the wrangler, resplendent in a new brown leather waistcoat, climb up on the stand and fiddle with the microphone. 'Well, folks, I think we're about ready to start.'

Chatter in the crowd died down.

'I'd like to introduce Whalen Cutter, our professional auctioneer, well known to many of you here.' A man in a quilted jacket made a deep bow, and people applauded politely.

'As well, we have Josh Mason, who will be leading the horses into the ring.'

Becky and Meg clapped and cheered. 'Josh has some fans in the stands, I see.' Cliff's grin was a mile wide. 'He's been gentling these horses so you can lead them right up into your trailers and take them home.'

Josh looked embarrassed but lifted his hat to the crowd.

'And finally, we have Wade Kovalchuk, who will be watching for you to raise those little brown squares of cardboard and indicate your bid to the auctioneer. You make sure he sees you!'

'That's Wade.' Meg tugged at Alison's sleeve. 'He's the bull-rider we were telling you about.'

Alison thought of making a sarcastic remark about how nice it was that both their boyfriends were there, but she was too heartsick to be sarcastic. She looked at the list in Meg's hand. The paint mares would be one of the last lots auctioned off. She would have to sit here through the whole thing.

Terri-Lyn could hear the sounds of the auction clearly from the open registration tent. They were getting through the list, selling some horses for pretty good prices, considering it was autumn, and people who bought them now would have to feed them over the winter. Hay was expensive with the drought.

The paints' lot number would be coming up soon. Terri felt sorry for Alison, sitting through this, but she was glad the girl had the grit to come. She thought she might just roll over in bed and refuse this morning.

The odd person was still arriving, looking for an auction ticket. Terri-Lyn wrote numbers on a few more, in case of last minute stragglers.

A big car was arriving now, a pretty strange vehicle for these parts – some kind of fancy taxi. A small, stooped woman got out, rummaged in her bag for sunglasses and headed for the seating.

'Oh, my lord,' Terri-Lyn breathed. 'If it isn't Grandmother Chant. What in blazes is she doin' here?'

She strode towards the benches to cut her off. If there was anyone Alison didn't need to see right now, it was her grandmother! Whatever punishment she deserved for telling lies, it couldn't include this.

'Excuse me, Ma'am,' she drawled in her best western way. 'Can I help you?'

'I'm looking for my granddaughter.' Grandmother Chant was peering up in the stands. She took no notice of Terri-Lyn.

'Well, Ma'am, you can't go up in the stands without a ticket. Let me assist you to our registration tent.' Terri-Lyn took her by the arm and propelled her forwards.

'What do you think you're doing?' Mrs Chant spluttered. 'Of all the outrageous . . .'

'Just trying to help, Ma'am.' They had reached the tent. 'Why, my gracious, I think I know you. Aren't you Mrs R. J. Chant, the famous New York socialite?' Terri-Lyn was pretty sure, that with her dark glasses in the shade of the tent,

Alison's grandmother didn't recognise her. It had been over sixteen years since they'd met.

'Well, yes, I am,' Grandmother Chant simpered.

'And what would you be doing, away out here in Wyoming?'

'Why, I often come to the spa at Jackson Hole,' Mrs Chant said. 'It's world famous, you know.'

'Oh, I do.' Terri-Lyn looked down, scribbling on a fictitious piece of paper. 'A lot of rich women go to that spa. We have a saying that the billionaires are buying out the millionaires in Jackson Hole, and the millionaires are messing up the rest of the state. You'd be one of those millionares, I suppose.'

'Well.' Grandmother Chant looked confused. She leaned forward. 'Confidentially, I'm also looking for my granddaughter, Alison Chant, who is staying in this area with a highly unsuitable relation.' Grandmother Chant's voice sank to a dramatic whisper. 'I was against her coming, but my daughter-in-law insisted.'

She sniffed, letting her listener know what she thought of her daughter-in-law. 'The child fell ill, as might have been expected in such wretched surroundings, and now I've seen her on national television, of all things. Apparently, this relation has talked her into purchasing a wild horse. Highly unsuitable for my granddaughter. She's a delicate child, and this whole rough, western riding is unsuitable. I've come to put a stop to it.'

'It's an awful long way to come, for someone of your age,' Terri-Lyn shook her head.

Grandmother Chant whipped off her glasses. 'My age?' She glared at Terri-Lyn, and then her face collapsed into a grimace of horror. 'Why you're . . . aren't you?'

'Terri-Lyn Arbus, at your service,' Terri grinned. 'It's been a long time, Mrs Chant. Nice to be remembered.'

'Why you. You strung me along. Where is my granddaughter?'

'Watching the auction, I figure.'

'I demand to see her. Give me that registration form.'

'Oh you don't need this, unless you intend to bid. Which I didn't gather that you did.'

'I insist you show me to my granddaughter.' Mrs Chant was shaking with fury.

'Right this way.' Terri-Lyn stood up slowly. She figured she had stalled as long as she could.

Chapter 19

LOT 43

It was time for the paints to be auctioned. Lot 43.

Alison sat hugging herself, as the two young mares came trotting into the ring. Josh had washed and groomed them. Their brown and white coats gleamed. Their beautiful manes and tails flowed around them as they ran. A lump formed in Alison's throat.

'Folks, you want some colour?' Cliff asked, his

voice booming into the microphone. 'Just take a look at these two young mares. They're gonna grow – have some size to them. Be real nice ridin' horses.' He glanced down at his papers. 'This first little horse, number 5719, she's had a bit of a cold. We're sellin' her as is, no guarantees, folks.'

The auctioneer took over. 'Anybody put $125 on this horse?'

There were no takers. The crowd sat silent. The two horses circled the ring.

Alison clenched her fists. Wasn't he at least going to offer them as a pair? If they were separated again, everything she'd done would be for nothing.

'All right, folks. Last chance.'

At that moment Alison saw her Grandmother Chant, zooming in like a bird of prey. She just had time to hear that horse number 5719 was a 'no sale' and would be held over for the next adoption. Then the old lady pounced.

'Grandmother! What are you doing here?'

This was the worst thing Alison could imagine.

'I've come to put a stop to all this nonsense about wild horses. I'm sure it was all her idea, that Terri-Lyn person.' She pointed at Terri-Lyn's retreating back.

'Where is she going?' Becky cried.

'She doesn't have the nerve to face me.' Mrs Chant poked at Becky. 'Would you move over and let me sit beside my granddaughter, please.' People behind were craning their necks, trying to see around the old woman. The bidding was about to start on the second mare in lot 43.

Becky reluctantly made room, and Mrs Chant squeezed in, clutching at Alison's arm. 'You see, it's quite easy to intimidate people of Terri-Lyn's sort,' she said. 'I just told her I had no intention of letting you buy one of these wild rough horses, and she caved in. Imagine the nerve of her, going on TV, telling the whole world she was buying you a horse, as if she was a person of importance in your life.'

Alison twisted out of her grandmother's grip.

'Grandmother,' she said through gritted teeth, 'Cousin Terri-Lyn was never going to bid on a horse for me. It was never true.'

'So she makes up stories for the TV? There, you see? What kind of a person does that?'

Alison stood up and glared down at her grandmother. 'Stop saying that stuff about Cousin Terri-Lyn. She's a good person – I made up the story, not her. And she is an important person in my life!'

'Alison!' Grandmother Chant said. 'You don't know what you're saying.'

'Oh, yes I do. I'm tired of all your rude comments about my mother's family. I don't want to hear any more of them, ever! I'm tired of you trying to bribe me and threaten me and push me around.'

'Hush! Not in public,' Grandmother Chant whispered hoarsely.

A tall person in a large black hat squeezed in

on the other side of Alison. 'Yes, hush!' she agreed. 'They're bidding on that horse, and I can't hear.' She held up a numbered card.

'Number 30 bids $150 on horse 5720. Thank you, Ma'am.' Josh pointed up at her.

'Cousin Terri-Lyn,' Alison gasped. 'What are you doing?'

'I'm bidding on this horse. Be quiet and let me pay attention.'

'She's a nice little mare. Do I hear $175?' bellowed the auctioneer.

There was silence in the benches.

'$150 once? Twice? SOLD to Ms Terri-Lyn Arbus.'

'I don't understand.' Alison stared at her,

'You aren't the only one who doesn't like getting pushed around,' Terri-Lyn grinned over at Grandmother Chant. 'I decided to go back and get a bidding card after all. Got back just in time to hear you saying all those nice things about me.'

'But what are you going to do with the horse?'

'We can work it out later. Let's just enjoy the rest of the auction and then we'll see what we can do about buying the other mare for $125. I think you said you had some of your birthday money left?'

There was a choking sound from Grandmother Chant.

Chapter 20

HEADING HOME

'Shadow is a good name for her,' Becky laughed. 'Look! She keeps as close to her friend as a shadow.'

Alison, Meg and Becky were gazing at the two horses from the fence the next morning. Alison was getting used to the idea that Shadow was really her horse, without feeling disloyal to Duchess. There would never be another Duchess, but Shadow needed her, and Alison had saved her life.

'Meg, what are you going to call your horse?' It had been decided between them that the older mare should be Meg's. That way, the two horses could stay together, and Meg could finally have a horse that was truly hers.

'I don't know what kind of name would suit her.' Meg reached through Terri-Lyn's pasture fence to stroke the mare's inquisitive nose with a loving hand. 'I can't believe she's really mine.'

'It should have something to do with her colouring,' Becky suggested. 'She's got that crazy patch over one eye, like somebody threw white paint at her.'

Meg's eyes lit up. 'How about Eye Patch? And I could call her Patch for short.'

'Great. Now they've got names,' Alison sighed. 'We just need a way to trailer them across the continent, a place to keep them, and money for food, vet bills and a thousand other things. Maybe it would be easier if we all stayed in Wyoming.'

'I like that idea.' Becky looked longingly at the surrounding hills. 'I hate the thought of going back east.'

'Oh no you don't.' Cousin Terri-Lyn came up behind them and put a hand on a shoulder of each of her cousins. 'I got the horses for you. It's up to you to figure out how to keep them. I can look after them for awhile, and I wouldn't even mind trekking them to New York – it would be worth the trip just to see the look on Roger Chant's face – but you're goin' home, and they're your horses, not mine.'

Her face crinkled into a laugh. 'Speaking of Roger, I guess your grandmother made it home all right yesterday?'

'She phoned and left a message with Mom,' Becky grinned. 'Mom said it scorched the phone, but Mrs Chant's fine.'

'Your mother will be here soon to pick you up.' Terri-Lyn looked at her watch. 'So say goodbye to your horses and pack up. I've had enough company for awhile.'

'Looks like you're getting more,' Alison said. A pickup was bumping down the long driveway, and it wasn't Becky's mom.

It was Josh and Wade, come to say goodbye. The five of them stood strung out along the fence, checking out the horses in their new home. 'Looks like they're settling in,' Josh said shyly. 'I'll start training them for you, if you like. It's good practise for me in my course at the college.'

'If you have time,' Alison said, 'that would be great. But I hope we can figure out a way to get them home soon. Meg and I kind of have our hearts set on training them ourselves.'

'Sure,' Josh nodded. 'Having seen you in operation I'll bet you can do it.'

'We might see you up in Calgary at the

Stampede,' Wade added. 'I'm gonna try to get good enough to compete in the bull riding up there next July, and Josh says he'll come too.'

Becky's face brightened. 'Maybe you could visit Mustang Mountain if you come to Alberta.'

'It would be nice to see you,' Meg agreed, looking at Wade. 'But I wish you'd find a safer event than riding bulls.'

'All right, enough. You boys skedaddle,' Terri-Lyn gave the order. 'These girls have to get packed up or they'll miss their plane.'

Half an hour later she folded all three of them in a mass hug. 'We had a good time, didn't we? Don't worry, I'll look after your horses.'

They piled into the pickup with Laurie's trailer behind, and set off down the long lane for the last time. 'I feel like I've been here a month instead of a week,' Meg sighed, looking back for a last glimpse of the horses.

At the airport, Laurie Sandersen kissed them goodbye. 'Good luck,' she told them. 'Stick together and think creatively. It will all work out.' She took Becky aside for a private hug. 'I'm going to miss you like crazy,' she said. 'But I'm glad you're going back with Alison. I have a feeling her parents aren't going to be happy about a wild horse.'

However, just two weeks later, Terri-Lyn received this e-mail :

Dear Cousin Terri-Lyn. We're writing this on Meg's computer for privacy reasons. It hasn't been easy, but we think we've got everything worked out for you to bring Shadow and Patch east whenever you can. This is how it works:

1. Virginia, the owner of Blue Barns, is not a snob, like we thought. It turns out she's crazy about wild horses

and she's all excited to board them in her stable.

2. Meg already has a job at Blue Barns that will pay for Patch's board, and surprise! Virginia wants me to help with the baby classes at the riding school. Me – a teacher!

3. My father is so happy about me having a job that he's agreed to let me keep Shadow. My mom agrees if she never has to drive us to the stable. Fine, we can take the bus.

4. My grandmother says no more birthday cheques, so I hope what was left is enough to pay for gas for the truck and hay for the horses.

So-o-o-If you can still bring them, I think we're ready. All of us are so excited to see you again and send our love and kisses to all the horses and Ross, the dog.

PS Say hi to Josh and Wade for Meg and Becky, and tell them we'll see them at the Calgary Stampede. PPS Meg says to tell you she's figured out you never really own a wild horse, they always belong to themselves. Do you think she's right?

Your loving great-cousin, Alison.

Step into the wild again as more drama and
danger await in the next Mustang Mountain
book . . .

Rodeo Horse

Here's a taste . . .

Chapter 1

FLYING CHANGE

Sara Kelly prepared for the run of her life. She knew her horse's heart was beating strongly, steadily between her knees. He loved to run, and he was ready to give her the best he had. Her own heart was beating just as madly, waiting for the buzzer that would set them off – through the chute and towards the first barrel.

It was December, at the Horner Creek Rodeo

near Calgary. Sara centred herself in the saddle, imagining a line running from the top of her head through her abdomen to her legs. A thousand-dollar scholarship if they won. Money for her first year of veterinary school, money she needed now that things were so bad on the ranch. Don't think about the ranch now! Sara told herself fiercely. Think about winning! Think about sending Sunny around those barrels perfectly and blazing for the finish line.

The buzzer sounded and the pounding of their hearts became the pounding of Sunny's hooves towards the first barrel. When they crossed the electric eye beam, the clock started running. Right turn around the first barrel, with Sunny in perfect position, his hind end powering him through the turn, then a flying lead change to the next barrel, around to the left. Once more a perfect turn, with Sara looking ahead to the final barrel at the top of the ring.

The next moment, Sara found herself flying

through the air as Sunny stumbled as he came out of the turn and pitched her over his head. She had no chance to regain her balance. She landed with her left leg twisted beneath her and felt something in her knee snap – then excruciating pain.

She could hear shouting as people raced towards her. She felt Sunny's muzzle in her face, smelled his warm horsey fragrance, but her eyes were squeezed shut with the effort of trying not to scream.

Sara knew what had happened to her. A ligament in her knee, badly torn in a skiing accident when she was twelve, had torn again.

But what had happened to Sunny? That was much more worrying. She would mend, despite the disgusting pain, but a horse with a badly broken leg . . . she tried to open her eyes to see him, but the pain was too great. Her head was spinning.

'Sara! Where are you hurt?' It was Lisa Rogers,

her friend and one of the people in charge of this rodeo. 'Can you hear me?'

Sara nodded and gripped her knee. 'How's Sunny?' she asked through clenched teeth.

'He looks OK.'

'Not limping?'

'Not that I can see. C'mon, how about you? Look at me, Sara.'

'I . . . can't, right now.' Sara fought off the waves of pain that made her stomach heave. Any slight movement made her want to howl. Now that she knew Sunny wasn't badly injured, there was no keeping that pain away.

'Stay still. The stretcher's coming. Hang on, kid. We'll have you out of here in no time. Hey! You should see how cute the ambulance guys are.'

Sara felt Lisa's hand on her shoulder and struggled to swallow the lump in her throat. She knew what this meant. A whole season of barrel racing down the drain. Weeks in a brace, on crutches, maybe surgery. Her dream of racing at the Calgary Stampede gone. And that meant no cash for college next autumn.

'It's OK, Sunny,' she whispered when he nickered unhappily near her ear. 'I know it wasn't your fault.' But what had gone wrong, she wondered? Sunny was usually so sure on his feet. What had brought her flying champion to such a sudden halt?

The ambulance attendants lifted Sara on the stretcher and carried her out of the ring. With her eyes closed and teeth gritted, she could hear the claps and cheers from the Horner Creek crowd.

EGMONT PRESS: ETHICAL PUBLISHING

Egmont Press is about turning writers into successful authors and children into passionate readers – producing books that enrich and entertain. As a responsible children's publisher, we go even further, considering the world in which our consumers are growing up.

Safety First
Naturally, all of our books meet legal safety requirements. But we go further than this; every book with play value is tested to the highest standards – if it fails, it's back to the drawing-board.

Made Fairly
We are working to ensure that the workers involved in our supply chain – the people that make our books – are treated with fairness and respect.

Responsible Forestry
We are committed to ensuring all our papers come from environmentally and socially responsible forest sources.

**For more information, please visit our website at
www.egmont.co.uk/ethical**

Mixed Sources
Product group from well-managed
forests and other controlled sources
www.fsc.org Cert no. TT-COC-002332
© 1996 Forest Stewardship Council

Egmont is passionate about helping to preserve the world's remaining ancient forests. We only use paper from legal and sustainable forest sources, so we know where every single tree comes from that goes into every paper that makes up every book.

This book is made from paper certified by the Forestry Stewardship Council (FSC), an organisation dedicated to promoting responsible management of forest resources. For more information on the FSC, please visit **www.fsc.org**. To learn more about Egmont's sustainable paper policy, please visit **www.egmont.co.uk/ethical**.